To Vic.

Smile often
Stay Beautiful
Life is unlimited!

By
Phil Farina

This is a work of fiction. Names, characters, places and incidents either are the product of the author's imagination or are used fictitiously. Any resemblance
to actual persons living or dead, events or locales is entirely coincidental.

FIRST EDITION 2018
Published in the United States of America

Author can be contacted at

pfarina@bex.net
Other Books by Phil Farina

Gravesend
The Enochian Dilemma

As always in any great work there are people who helped in the creative process, this work has many.

First, I want to thank my wife Cathy, for her support during the entire process. She kept me going, reading, editing and making suggestions. She is the love of my life.

My cousin Linda, provided inspiration, moral support and helped shape the final story. I truly appreciate her help.

To my beta readers, thank you for your thoughts, your ideas, and especially your criticism. Without you this book would never have seen the light of day.

To my cover designer, Tony Barone, thank you for once again creating a stunning cover.

Finally, to my editor Carol Hoenig, I thank you for your comments, suggestions and overall support.

And to you all, my readers. Thank you for your support. I hope this book brings you a little joy and opens your minds to possibilities outside the bounds of what we can see and hear.

Thank you all and enjoy!

GHOST WITCH

A Skadegamutc, or Ghost-Witch,

is said to be born from the dead body of a medicine man who practiced black magic. The spirit of the Skadegamutc refuses to stay dead and, after death, retains a powerful evil, magic energy that allows him to return to this world and come to life only at night to kill, eat, and throw curses at any unlucky humans who come across him. The only way to permanently destroy a Ghost Witch is to destroy their evil energy.

Native American Lore

"Legend says that the guardians of the spirit world lived in the rocks and the trees and that one day, they're going to come back into our world to destroy us."
Hopi Prophecy

Preface

I am Shingas, born in the light of an age when we, The People, ruled over the land. We were one with the spirit. Mother Nature (Kahesena Haki) was my true mother, the Great Spirit (Kitanitowit) my true Father, and the winds my true brother (Xansati). My mother taught me the lessons of the four kingdoms, and I learned to walk the path she had chosen so long ago.

I grew strong among my people, The Lenni Lenape. I followed the path to the spirit world where I became a medicine man (metina), strong of character and wise in the art. I was true to the magic. I called upon my mother and the four winds to help me keep my people safe and strong. We were peaceful, living as one with the land.

I listened to the song of my brother, the East Wind (Wehenchiopank Wentxen) and learned the knowledge of the grandfathers. The legends of my people taught me the ways of my ancestors and, through this knowledge, I learned wisdom through illumination.

From the South Wind (Shaonaxen), I learned the ways of questioning; always seeking the truth. As I learned the truth, I grew in strength and stature as I continued to travel along the chosen path. I grew strong as I lived the truth and nature was always with me.

From the West Wind (Eheliwsikakw Wentxen), my wisest brother, I learned responsibility, not only to my fellow man, but to love and respect the mother in all things. The earth, the winds, the water, the animals were all part of the Great Being (Linkweheleokan) and must be respected by The People.

And finally, from the fierce North Wind (Luwanaxen), where the elders dwell, I learned to live in harmony and to walk in balance with man and nature. I learned renewal, not only of the land but of my spirit and the ways of my people. From this I was able to be pure in mind, body and spirit. I grew in strength and wisdom and followed the path long into my life.

I learned all these things as the Great Spirit guided me and so I became the Great Medicine Man (Meteina Kanshawen), first of my kind, for my people. At first, I followed the chosen path. I lived in the light. I worked with The People to bring balance to our family, to live in harmony with the mother and the father and the brother winds. I was at peace in my heart and mind. My soul soared with the eagle and swam with the bear. I was strong and kind in all things. I healed the sick, breathed life into the newly born and helped the dying move on to the spirit world. Peace and harmony were my guides. I thanked the mother each day for the blessings she gave to The People.

This, however, was not to last. The peace The People felt changed in an instant. They came with their beads, and their guns. They replaced harmony with war. They brought gifts and disease. They preached their God and disrespected our gods. Mother Nature was something to abuse; so, they stole from her very heart the gifts she gave The People and they returned nothing. The land was scarred, the water fouled, the air polluted. Our people decimated.

I too changed. I became darkness itself. I learned to practice the black arts, to wield spells and mix potions, to rid us of this evil incarnate that spread like a pestilence upon the land. But there were too many. They came in ships, built settlements, and encroached upon our hunting grounds as so many rats invade the grain stores. My people, The People of the Lenni Lenape, once proud, who had lived in balance and harmony were gone. I too was gone, but I was strong in life and so remained strong in death.

As I lay dead upon the bier, high above the land I loved so much, my heart prayed to the mother, "Do not let me die in vain, but let me live in the darkness; let me bring suffering to those who brought much pain and death to our people. Let me dwell in their dark hearts and strike from within." And so, my prayer was answered.

I am Shingas, Great Medicine Man of the Lenni Lenape and a Ghost Witch.

Chapter 1

They were the perfect family and, as such, would be the first to die.

Rick was a thirty-something self-taught computer genius. He was employed at his ideal position as Director of Research and Development for a small, but up and coming, computer company headquartered in New England. Fortunately, Rick and his wife Alla were able to remain in New Brunswick, right near his boyhood home due to the marvels of telecommuting.

Rick loved everything computer. Growing up, he drove his parents to distraction, forever building and then burning up computers and computer parts. His childhood goal was to build the fastest, most powerful computer ever designed. He burnt up many motherboards, fried uncountable hard drives and even accidentally set fire to his room in his quest for perfection.

His father once said to him, "Son, there is so much electrical diffusion in this room I think you are going to make yourself sterile." The birth of the twins years later proved Rick was anything but sterile.

Rick met his future wife in high school. They were in the same class where Alla tried to study German while Rick studied the cute Russian girl in the front of the room. Let's just say Rick was not much into academics but was really into Alla.

Unfortunately for high school hormones, Alla was "dating" another young man. Her dating was not going all that well, so she soon befriended Rick who lent a most needed soft shoulder for Alla to bemoan all the failures of her current beau. Rick only had to lend an ear and wait to win the girl.

Although Rick and Alla went to the senior prom together at the end of high school, he assured everyone they were just friends. They had a great time and soon parted ways when Alla went off to college and Rick attended a different academy of higher learning. They stayed in touch, visiting during holidays when they both came back to New Brunswick.

Their friendship remained strong and soon blossomed into something more, much more, when Alla visited Rick after yet another breakup. Rick and Alla soon learned that dating your best friend was much better than dealing with a stranger. One thing led to another and to another and so on until they were married, much to the delight of friends and family. Everyone knew it was the perfect marriage, so it too would be the perfect tragedy.

In their first few years of marital bliss, Alla worked for a well-known international company that made electric switches. She quickly moved up in the organization due to her own computer skills, supported and encouraged by the ever-helpful genius at home. She soon was head of her own department.

The pair spent their first few years living frugally in a nice but small apartment, simple but comfortable furniture, most scrounged from other people's houses. It seemed that Rick "borrowed" the family room from the basement of his parent's home to get the apartment more comfortable. They added a few tables and chairs and, of course, the biggest flat screen TV money could buy. After all, they had their priorities.

After several years, the desire emerged to start a family. Rick and Alla wanted a family of two children, preferably a boy and a girl, just to keep with perfection. So, it was decided before they would start a family, they should buy a home in a safe neighborhood, with a great school system, on a side road with enough room in the backyard to be filled with yard toys and a pool for the growing family.

It didn't take long for the pair to fall deeply in love with their future home. Just east of downtown New Brunswick, in an area called Westons Mills, lay a beautifully designed neighborhood of pricey, single family homes. The neighborhood was a well-planned community. There was a neighborhood swimming pool, tennis courts and a community center surrounded by a lovely park setting where kids could play on their own while remaining safely within earshot of their ever-watchful parents.

The area was bounded on the north by the historic Raritan River, a calm scenic waterway, replete with boat docks, canoeing and sailboat rentals. The swiftly moving water was the home of a fish population that included largemouth bass, smallmouth bass, sunfish, catfish, trout, chain pickerel, American eels, carp and yellow perch. Pike can be found in relative abundance in some portions of the river, perfect for a boy and his father to enjoy.

Also, along the Raritan River was a section of land, about 100 acres, set aside as the Raritan River Conservancy, designed to conserve and protect the waterway. This patch of wild land, once part of the Lenni Lenape Tribal lands, lent itself to a beautiful view of the river and protected the local homes from flooding on the rare occasion when the river crested above the gently sloping banks.

The happy couple found a beautiful split level four- bedroom home, with a full finished basement, perfect for an at home office for Rick, with plenty of excess play room for the budding family. The backyard was deep, about 200 feet, and made even larger by the fact that it bordered the conservancy. They would have the luxury of having access to a huge piece of land without having to pay the huge New Jersey taxes associated with having a huge tract of land. They could also access the river directly from their backyard by walking a short distance through the conservancy. It was perfect.

In no time at all, the pair moved in and made the home comfy-cozy. They still lived frugally, having brought with them some of their old furniture. The borrowed parents' furniture was well worn and past its prime, so it was discarded, only to be replaced by furniture given to them by Rick's maternal grandmother, which she purchased some forty-five years earlier.

Soon the pair set out to make the house their home. They painted the walls in subdued hues, added new rugs, changed the kitchen to accommodate a more modern styling and purchased a new addition to the entertainment center, which now included the largest 3D flat screen TV money could buy. Again, they had their priorities.

Once the house was settled and Rick was moving up the corporate ladder, it was time to start a family. After five years as a couple, they hoped to welcome their first child.

Well, sometimes things do not go as planned. Alla was soon expecting. Everyone was happy to hear the news. As things progressed, the mother- to- be seemed to be getting larger and larger. They soon found out why: twins. Alla was having twins.

Delighted at the prospect, the pair set out setting up the nursery to accommodate two little bundles of joy. They didn't know, however, if they should be preparing a color palate for a boy or a girl. It was a bit perplexing, but the doctor was able to shed some light on the issue. During a routine sonogram exam, the doctor asked if the couple wanted to know the sex of the babies. In unison, Rick and Alla said yes and the doctor revealed the surprise. "One of each" he said. They would have their perfect family.

On June 18, Rick and Alla welcomed Alaric and Kenzie into the family.

Chapter 2

The next four years were filled with the dreams and tensions of raising twins. Alaric, the eldest by a full twenty-nine minutes, and Kenzie were inseparable. They did everything together: they got sick together, they learned potty training together, and they even developed their own language, much to the chagrin of their parents. They would happily talk all day to each other, laughing and pointing at their parents. Each child had that devilish twinkle in their eyes.

Despite the trials and tribulations of parenthood, Alla and Rick were the proudest of doting parents. The children were beautiful in every way and life was good.
That would change soon.

One of the reasons Rick wanted this particular house was that it lent itself perfectly to someday adding an inground pool in the back yard, complete with patio, barbeque pit, and a hot tub in the corner of the pool.

On June 18th, the twins' fourth birthday, construction started on the pool. Kenzie was inside helping momma bake cookies. "Choco bits," she said as she dumped in the chips, getting more on the counter than in the bowl. Alaric was in heaven as the construction team brought in a backhoe to dig the ground out. He spent the better part of two solid days standing in the back yard, describing every action by the backhoe. He was in heaven.

'Now, the man is going to drop the digger in the ground and pull up the dirt and drop it in the big truck," he would squeal with delight to his father. Rick had his hands full trying to keep Alaric from running to the backhoe and climbing in.

One time the driver saw Alaric pointing at the equipment and he called out, "Hey, young man, want a ride?" Before Rick could stop him, little Alaric was running at top speed right for the hole. Rick grabbed him in the nick of time and was able to guide the squealing child around the hole and into the cab of the backhoe.

Alaric sat in the cab on the man's lap. He let him pull the lever to stretch out the arm. Then he showed him how to pull back on the same lever to bite into the earth and pull out a full bucket. Alaric talked about how he "dug the hole for the pool all by himself" to anyone who would listen.

The time came for dinner and Alaric thanked the driver for "the best day ever," and father and son headed into the house to clean up from a hard day's work.

As the construction worker was putting the backhoe away for the night, he noticed something down in the hole. It looked like a white rock, but it was oddly shaped. Getting closer to examine the odd rock, the worker soon learned that it wasn't a rock at all, but a human skull.

Where the hell did this come from? he thought to himself.

Now, New Jersey has some tough laws concerning desecration of a grave site and even more laws governing what you can and can't do if you find human bones at a construction site. The worker climbed down a little deeper in the hole and looked around, searching for, and hoping not to

17

find any more bones. With no more bones in sight and the digging complete, the worker decided not to say anything to anyone; he didn't want to lose the contract and end up tearing up the whole yard looking for some more old bones. He figured what no one knows couldn't hurt anyone. Wrong.

He climbed out of the hole with the skull wrapped in a cloth, so no one would see what he had. Quickly, he headed back to the truck, pulled out an old bag that was lying in the cab, and threw the skull, rag and all, into it. He looked around, conspiratorially, just to make sure no one saw him. He carried the bag casually to the curb and dumped it in the garbage can. Tomorrow was garbage day and the skull would be gone with no one the wiser. He wiped his hands on his bandana, wiped the bandana across his brow, jumped in the truck, and headed off home. Little did he know the death and havoc he would unleash.

Chapter 3

The next weekend, Alla and her mother, Rita, were off on their monthly shopping trip to the mall in Woodbridge. They would often go to lunch, shop for hours, maybe take in a matinee, and be home for a late dinner; just to get away from the twins for a few hours and to spend time with her mother.

Rick, on the other hand, was at home with the twins, a job he relished as he could sometimes act four years old himself. It seemed that when MOMMY was gone, the three kids were free to play and play they did.

Kenzie was at the age when a tea party was the highlight of her day. Both Dad and Alaric were not as thrilled as they could be, but they suffered through, as Kenzie set the play table with her best plastic tea set, put out some cookies that mommy and she made that morning, and poured "tea" from her prized tea pot into tiny cups.

Dad and Alaric sat on the floor, belly up to the tiny table, and enjoyed tea and "biscuts" as mispronounced by the affable Kenzie.

Once tea time was over, play time began. And play they did. First it was a game of tag outside. Kenzie and Alaric ran around squealing "not me, nooooooo" as the big mean daddy acted like a troll, trying to catch the kids so he could "eat them up." Even the old dog, Iris, got in on the act, running and barking and chasing the kids, trying to help protect them from the troll.

Although the kids loved this game, for Rick there was an ulterior motive. If he could tucker them out running around the backyard, he could feed them lunch and hopefully put them down for a nap, so he could get some work done. Most times this worked out well, and today was no exception.

After a good hour running around outside, playing tag, climbing on the jungle gym Rick built last summer, and swinging on the swings, everyone was pooped.

"Time to go inside for lunch," Rick announced. The twins raced inside, led by Iris.

"Okay, who wants what to eat?"

"I wanna peebutter and jewee samich," announced Kenzie with glee. It was her favorite.

"Gwapes, cawrots, cheese, and coocumbers," Alaric announced as he squinted he eyes and shook his head with glee. Rick said to himself, *what is wrong with that boy?*

Lunch was made by Chef Daddy, delivered on paper plates. There was always the danger of an accident if they used real plates.

The first thing Kenzie did was smash her peebutter and jewee sandwich. She laughed as the jelly flew off the plate and onto the table. Dad, on the other hand, delivered that stern look that said, without words, was that really necessary?

Lunch was soon over, and the twins helped daddy clean up by taking their nearly empty plates to the trash and finishing their mango juice.

They were all pooped, and Rick ushered them to bed for a nap. Most of the time they slept in their separate rooms, a rule administered by the mean Mommy, but when Daddy was in charge, the twins would share a bed.

'Okay, guys, where are we napping today?"
"The car. I wanna sleep in the car!" announced Kenzie. It seems that Alaric had a bed that was in the shape of a car while Kenzie had one in the shape of a princess castle.

"Okay, Alaric, can Kenzie sleep with you in the car?" Rick knew full well Alaric would jump at the chance to sleep in his own bed with Kenzie.

"Yes, yes, the car," they both responded and bounded off down the hall toward Alaric's room. After a few minutes and one bedtime story about diggers, for Alaric, and one about puppies for Kenzie, it was time to close the door and take a much-needed nap.

"Okay, guys, not a peep from this room," Rick said, knowing full well it would take them half an hour of twin chat before they would fall asleep.

Once they were down, Rick set out to do some work in his office. Three hours later, the twins woke up. It was a little after four. Alla was expected to be home around six and the crew would be off to their favorite pizza parlor for Saturday night pizza family fun.

With two hours to kill, Rick fed the twins a lite snack of grapes, cheese and, of course, one "choco bits" cookie each. Now, it was time for the twins' favorite game of hide and seek.

In this game, daddy was always the seeker and the twins were always the hiders. Rick would go into the master bedroom, sit on the bed, close his eyes and count to twenty, while the twins would go yelling and screaming around the house trying to find the "bestest" place to hide.

Alaric would almost always hide in the kitchen cabinet under the sink. It was a tight squeeze, but he would manage quite well. So, like always, he crawled into the cabinet, shut the door and tried to be quiet. Kenzie was a little more inventive. She would sometimes hide under the pile of clothes in the laundry room, or even lay down in the bath tub. Today, she chose the laundry.

While Rick was sitting on the bed in the dark with his eyes closed, a rule set by the twins, he felt a little funny. He couldn't explain exactly what was happening; he just felt a bit dizzy for a second or two. Suddenly, he felt a very sharp pain in his temples. "What the...?" he said as he put both hands to his temples and fell back on the bed. For a brief terrifying moment, he thought he was having a stroke. Too bad it wasn't.

The pain swelled and pulsed until he felt as if his head were cracking open. Something was terribly wrong. Then, just as suddenly as it started, it stopped. The pain was gone, replaced by something worse, much worse.

Rick sat there on the bed. He opened his eyes and was going to rub his temple to shake out the last of the pain, but he couldn't move his hands. *Oh my God! What the hell is happening to me?* Sweat began forming on his forehead, dripping down into his eyes. Suddenly, he stood up and turned around the room, as if seeing it for the first time.

Something was terrifyingly wrong. He was not in control of his body. It was as if someone, or something, had taken control over his physical form, but left his mind alone. He was able to see what was happening, but powerless to stop it. Rick was terrified.

He turned again, or rather his body turned again, around the room and he heard a voice in his head say in a very guttural tone, but almost like singing or chanting, "I have returned."

Now, if there is a stage past terrified, Rick was there. His body moved forward, out of his control, and entered the hallway. The voice said again, "I have returned, and vengeance is mine." And so, it was.

Rick could not control his actions, yet he could see and hear everything that took place. By the time the carnage was complete, there was blood everywhere. Rick tried to fight whatever was controlling his body, but nothing he did had any effect. It was as if he were in the audience of a horror movie, a witness to what happened and yet unable to warn the actors.

When the action was over, he felt as if his head was about to split apart. He fell to the floor, rolling on the bloody carpet, holding his head in both hands, screaming in excruciating pain. Suddenly, he felt as if something left his body. He regained full control of his arms and legs. Slowly, carefully, trying to regain his balance, he stood up. He looked around and was immediately sickened at the scene around him. He retched uncontrollably adding to the horrors surrounding him.

As he looked toward the north, he could see, or thought he could see, something floating in the corner about three feet above the floor. He could not make out what it was, but he imagined he could see a face in the center of the swirling mass. The face was smiling at him. Knowing that the entity was what took over his body, Rick screamed, "Who are you and what have you done?"

"It is not what I have done, it is what you and your kind have done. I am Shingas and I have come to avenge my people." At this the shadow figure rushed at Rick, who tried to backpedal to escape the attack, but he was unsteady and tripped over the scatter rug in front of the fireplace. He fell forward, hitting his head on the corner brick, splitting it open like a ripe watermelon.

The entity stayed for a moment to enjoy his work and then vanished into the winds.

At precisely six p.m., Alla walked into the house and called out, "Hi, guys! Mommy's' home. There was normally a flurry of activity as the twins raced from wherever they were to greet her. Even Iris would rise from wherever she was sleeping to greet her mistress. But today there was nothing, only silence, and the strange smell of iron.

Alla reached the top of the steps and screamed in horror at the sight before her. Before she could move another step, she felt an unseen hand roughly push against her chest and she tumbled head-over-heels, down the steps, hitting the back of her head, breaking her neck, and killing her instantly.

Chapter 4

Three days later, the call came into the 911 desk at the New Brunswick police department on Kirkpatrick Street.

"911, what is your emergency?" Carol, a five-year veteran of the Emergency Call Center, asked, following the script.

"I don't really have an emergency," came the reply from a harried and upset Rita, "but I have not heard from my daughter and son-in-law in several days. I call and call and there is no answer. I am so worried," she continued, not giving Carol a chance to chime in. "I am so worried. Can you send someone to the house to check on them?"

"Calm down, Miss…?"

"Rita, my name is Rita. My daughter is Alla and her husband is Rick. I am so worried; I cannot reach them, and I have no car. Oh, please, can you send someone?" Carol had seen this dozens of times in the past. The kids go off on a spur of the moment three-day weekend and scare the hell out of Grandma, who calls the police. Normally, Carol would blow this off, but Rita seemed really distraught and it was a slow day. Carol was sure she could call out to the patrols in the area and someone could do a house check and see that all is okay.

Carol said, "I will send out a patrol just to make sure everyone is all right. Can you give me the address, please?"

"Thank you. Thank you. Thank you," replied Rita, then gave the address. "Please have them call me. I am worried half to death."

"I am sure everything is fine," Carol said in her calming voice. "I am sure they will call you soon."

Carol filled a cup of coffee, her fourth of the day, before she put out the call on the radio. "Any available units in the area of Westons Mills, I need a house check. Any units, please respond."

Detectives Paul Mercuri and Dave Delair were just finishing lunch at Tumulty's Pub, their favorite stop for the best burgers in town. The pub was located on George Street in New Brunswick, a short three miles to the address Carol called out over the radio. Paul and Dave normally would never take a house check call, but it was a real slow day, and they had just finished their last big homicide case, so they felt that a house check was just the way to kill an hour.

"This is unit 21, responding to the house check," called Paul over the radio as the senior detective, Dave, pulled out of the parking lot and into light traffic.

"Hey, boys, isn't a house check below two big time detectives who just cleared their big case?" Carol chided.

"Well, Carol, for you we will just drop everything and mosey on over and see what's what," replied Paul, chuckling a little over the radio.

"Oh, thank you so much. I feel privileged."

"Don't mention it, 21 out," replied Paul as he hung the mike back on the dash hook.

Turning to his partner, he said, "Nothing like a routine stop to get the old body back in the swing."

"I hope you're right," kidded Dave. "You never know anymore what you will find, routine or not."

Three minutes later they pulled up in their unmarked black Ford Avenger, the kind you could tell a mile away was a cop car. Dave got out of the driver's side and said to Paul as he jumped out of the passenger side, "You take the front door and I'll head around back and check it out. See anything, call me on the radio."

"No problemo." Paul headed toward the front door.

Detective Paul Anthony Mercuri was born in New York City and, at the ripe old age of twenty-two, joined the force of New York City's finest. He started out, as they all do, as a beat cop. After seven years on the force, the twenty-nine-year-old had seen enough of the horrors of New York and decided to move across the river to New Jersey where he was hired as a detective in New Brunswick. After another five years of service, he was promoted to Homicide Detective and introduced to the worst side of people once again.

Detective Dave Delair, ten years older than Paul, was a New Jersey boy through and through. Born in Piscataway, a suburban town north of downtown New Brunswick, he attended Rutgers College in Newark where he studied criminology. From there it was directly to the New Brunswick

Police force, then up the ranks until he was a Senior Homicide Detective. The two had been partners for three years and were so close they seemed to use telepathy to communicate.

As Detective Mercuri headed up the driveway to the front door, his police sense kicked in. There were two cars in the driveway, yet there was a two-car garage. It was unusual, since in this neighborhood, people usually parked in the garage, but not out of the ordinary either. The front yard was well kept, except for the newspapers piling up on the front porch. He took a quick look at the dates as he climbed the cement porch steps and noticed that, since Sunday, the paper had not been collected. Again, unusual, but not alarming. Maybe the family headed out for a three-day adventure and forgot to stop the paper. But why were both cars in the driveway? Alone, these points were not an issue; taken together, however, his Spidey sense kicked up a notch.

Detective Delair headed around back and noticed a well-kept yard, groomed flower bed, and fenced in backyard. He opened the gate, which was well-oiled, so it didn't make a sound, and noticed the backyard had a pool, which looked rather new; a jungle gym, swings, and other paraphernalia one would expect to see in a home with children.

As he walked toward the sliding door, Dave just barely escaped stepping into a pile of dog poop. Ok, so they had a dog. Hoping it was friendly, he investigated the house through the sliding glass door.

As his eyes adjusted to the dim light inside, he was slightly alarmed at the scene within. Nothing really looked out of

29

sorts, but there was smear of what looked like blood on the floor. Drawing his weapon with one hand, he keyed the mike on his radio. "Paul, head back here. There is something on the floor; I think it's blood."

"Roger that," replied Paul as he, too, drew his weapon and headed at a trot to back up his partner.

"Mercuri, take a look in there and tell me what you see."

Paul peeked around the side of the door, trying not to be seen by whoever might be inside while trying to get a good look himself.

Paul stepped back, looked at his partner, and whispered, "Looks like blood to me and a lot of it.
Should we call for back-up?"

"Not yet. Let's see if we can get in first and have a look around. Looks to me like the scene is a few days old, so I doubt a perp is still inside"

"Roger that, after you." Paul made a show of bowing and gesturing with his hand, the universal gentlemanly gesture of, "You first."

Dave rolled his eyes and reached out with one hand, holding his weapon at the ready with the other and slid the door open. It wasn't locked.

Careful not to step in the blood, so as not to contaminate the scene, he passed through the door and entered the dining room. There was no one in the room, but there was a smell, an overbearing smell of something foul. It was a smell Detective Delair had smelled many times before, the smell of death.

His gun raised, pointing toward the ceiling, Delair stepped through the dining room and turned left toward the family room. That was when Veteran Detective Dave Delair contaminated the crime scene by regurgitating his double cheeseburger from Tumulty's Pub.

Chapter 5

For the next few days the crime scene was a flurry of activity.
Officers from CSI came and went. Cleaning crews, replete
with Tyvek suits, cleaned the blood and reporters hung
around, hoping to get a glimpse of something. What, no one
knew. The whole scene was rung with yellow POLICE LINE
DO NOT CROSS tapes as a constant reminder of what
horrors were within.

Detectives Mercuri and Delair tried to write a police report,
but every time they sat down to write, the horrors of the
scene flooded in. Finally, Paul told Dave, "Go home, you look
dogged. Get some rest and let me give it a try."

"You don't have to tell me twice," Dave replied, grabbing his
things and making a beeline for the door.

Paul sat down, scooted his desk chair toward the keyboard,
cracked his fingers, and typed. The report described in
minute detail the scene of the crime. *Upon entering the back-
sliding glass door, the responding officers noticed a trail of blood
leading from the back door across the dining room and into the
living room. By the shape and the smearing of blood, the officers
presumed that someone or something was dragged through the area.
Following the trail, the responding officers found a female dog lying
on its side, partially eviscerated from what appeared to be a large
gut wound.*

*Proceeding along the blood trail, the lead officer came into the family
room. Immediately visible were the remains of three victims. One
victim was an adult male of about thirty years old, his head split*

open on the corner of the brick fireplace. The two other victims appeared to be young children, no older than four years of age."

The young victims had been brutally attacked by an, as yet, unknown assailant. There were pools of blood surrounding each victim, without signs of smearing, indicating that the victims had not been moved once deceased. The floors, walls, and ceiling were covered in blood splatter, indicative of a brutal and violent attack. The male child seemed to have severe lacerations about the arms and legs with additional deep stab wounds over his back and chest. There were no defensive marks immediately visible, possibly indicating a rapid attack or the victim knew his attacker. The female child was a few feet away toward the fireplace and suffered the same wounds.

Examination of the adult male victim showed no apparent stab wounds or lacerations, only a massive head wound, apparently caused when the victim hit his head on the corner fireplace brickwork with enough force to split his head open. Brain matter and blood were splattered on the brickwork and floor. The wound was apparently immediately fatal.

The responding officers continued toward the front door where a fourth victim, an adult female, was found deceased at the bottom of the steps. It appeared the victim fell backwards down the steps, possibly breaking her neck. There were no other wounds apparent; nor was there any blood near the victim.

Upon closer inspection there was one oddity to the scene. The two young victims appeared to have tear wounds over the left carotid artery, as if they had been bitten post mortem. It also looked like the blood splatter surrounding the young victims appeared to be *smeared, as if it were lapped up by some animal. No other victims were present.*

Paul pushed back from his desk, pulled the report from the printer, read it, signed it, then quickly put it in his out basket, hoping to forget what he saw.

Unfortunately, the next scene would be worse, much worse.

Chapter 6

The next few days were an exercise in frustration for the embattled detectives. They went over every aspect of the case. They visited the crime scene three times. They walked every inch of the house, observing, taking notes, asking more and more questions. "What happened here?" "Who did it?" "Why?" And most frustrating, "Where the hell did they come from and where did they go?"

They spent hours scouring the scene. They took hundreds of photos; collected samples of every surface associated with the crime and asked a hundred questions of the neighbors. They even tracked down the mailman, the newspaper boy, and poor Rita. Over and over, they analyzed the data, and, for all their efforts, they were no further along than when they started.

They had bupkis.

"We gotta be missing something," said Paul grumbling, while sitting at his desk across from his partner. He ran his hand through his dark hair and shook his head in frustration as he pored over the data. "There has to be one clue. One damn clue. We just don't see it."

Dave was equally frustrated. "Okay, so here's what we know so far. There are four bodies."

"Five, if you count the dog," corrected Paul

"Okay, five bodies. Four of which were killed in a most gruesome way. Two were killed by stab wounds over their entire torso, and the dog was split open."

"Right so far"

"The adult male, however, showed no stab wounds. He died when he fell and hit his head on the fireplace brick splitting his head open. He was covered in the victim's blood and near his right hand was the murder weapon, a large Cutco butcher knife, confirmed by the lab rats," Dave continued.

"Okay, I'm with you so far."

"So, here is what I got. The male goes on a rampage, kills the kids, then the wife comes home. There's a struggle, the wife falls down the stairs, the husband falls back and hits his head. Both dead, case closed."

"Tell me, Dave, do you really buy that for a second?"

"NO! Damn it, but what the hell else do we have?" replied Dave, striking his desk with his hand. "What the hell else do we have?"

"Nothing, man. Nothing."

It was one week later that they had something, but it wasn't what they'd hoped for.

Chapter 7

It was a beautiful sunny July morning, just a perfect day for the Fourth of July celebrations. The sun was shining, and the temperature was going to hit a comfortable eighty degrees, with low humidity, just a perfect day for a family picnic in the back yard.

Joseph and Katherine had been married for all of five years; they had a son, Anthony, of two and a "bun in the oven." They were young and in love and just starting out on the long road to happiness.

The two met at Xavier University in Cincinnati, Ohio as undergraduates. Katherine was studying art and Joseph was studying linguistics in preparation for applying to medical school. It seems that medical schools were looking for well-rounded applicants, hence the nonbiology route to med school.

One thing led to another and Joseph proposed to Katherine in his senior year. She accepted, and the wedding was less than a year later. Joseph lost interest in medical school when he saw his uncle, a doctor in Buffalo, sacrifice home and family for a medical career. Joseph did not want that kind of life, so he decided to refocus his career path. After a few years of odd jobs in the Pittsburgh market, where Katherine grew up, Joseph applied to USC and was accepted into the PhD program for linguistics. Gone was the notion of medical school in favor of the academic life.

Katherine turned her art degree into a nice little business in printing. Joseph bought her a small letterpress printer and soon DPK Printing was born where she designs various invitations, stationery and other traditional, yet unique, printed items. They were the picture-perfect couple.

"Hey, Joseph," Katherine called from the back door, "are you and Anthony ever going to stop digging?"

"Someday soon, I hope," Joseph called back.

Joseph and his helper, Anthony, were in the backyard, installing an in-ground sprinkler system. Joseph loved to work outside, since his day job as a Professor at Rutgers University kept him cooped up in either a classroom or an office all day. He was a newly minted PhD from USC. He and his wife enjoyed the academic life, although they were a bit on the formal side, never calling each other by nicknames, they still enjoyed life to the fullest.

Joseph just could not wait for summer, so he could work outside in the yard. He had already finished installing the sprinkler system in the front last year, designed a beautiful bird bath with a fountain for the backyard, and planted trees, bushes, and flowers throughout the property. It was one of the nicer looking landscapes in the Westons Mills neighborhood.

They lived at the corner of Wilcox and Halstead, and their backyard bordered the Raritan River conservancy. The home was perfect for raising a family of four, "or more" as Katherine often put it. The backyard was large, and the added view of the conservancy added much to their privacy. A split rail fence kept Anthony confined without compromising the view. "Guys, you need to clean up, if you want to have a picnic and be ready for the fireworks tonight," Katherine called to the digging crew.

"One more hole and we're done for today," Joseph called back as Anthony dug his tiny shovel into the dirt at his father's feet. "More hole," he echoed.

Joseph laughed at his son and picked up his shovel and started to dig the last hole of the day. About two feet into the soft loamy ground, he struck something, hard. He pulled out the shovel, plunged it into the ground, and once again struck something. It did not make the shovel ring as a rock would. It was more like a "crack" sound, as if it broke through something.

Dropping the shovel, he fell to his knees and began to dig with his hands in the soft warm soil. Soon he felt something hard, dug a little deeper, and pulled up an object.

At first, he didn't know what he was holding. It was about a foot long, covered in dirt, and looked odd for sure. He had a bottle of water nearby. Joseph always had water nearby as he was a fanatic water drinker, and he used it to wash off the object. As soon as the dirt fell off, he was horrified to discover he was holding a bone in his hand. From all accounts, it looked like a human bone.

"Daddy, what that?" Anthony asked as Joseph dropped the water bottle to get a better look at the bone.

"Nothing, pal," he assured Anthony, who went immediately back to digging his own hole.

Reverently, Joseph placed the bone on the ground and investigated the hole to see what else might be in there. It was deep and dark, so he swallowed hard and stuck his hand deep into the soil. He felt around a bit, relieved to feel nothing, but dirt for a moment. Just as he was about to pull his hand out, he felt something else, smooth and hard. His heart skipped a beat. He hoped against hope that the bone was an anomaly, but he soon dug up another and another. Four bones in all. Joseph had no idea why there were bones there, but they looked old, really old. Unfortunately, he was all too familiar with what happens when a construction site finds bones anyplace in New Jersey. The city sends in an archeology team and they dig up everything. Not wanting to have his yard and all his hard work ruined by a bunch of "bone hunters," he put the bones in a bucket. Then, he brought Anthony inside, telling Katherine, "I have to put something away. Wash this rug rat clean. By then I'll be done, and we can get on with the picnic."

"Come on, muddy boy, let's get you cleaned up." Katherine took Anthony inside, leaving Joseph alone for a moment.

He took his bucket of bones, walked out the back gate into the conservancy area, headed to the river, and tossed the bones, one by one, as far as he could into the river. He reached down into the river with the bucket, filled it with water, swirled it around and tossed the water back into the river taking with it any remains left in the bucket. He stood there for a moment looking out over the rushing water. He thought he might have heard a cry. Something like the sound one might make when they were in horrible pain. Something from deep within. He stood there a little longer, straining to see if he would hear it again, but nothing. The silence was broken by the cry of the birds swooping in and out of the water hunting for small minnows. *Must be time for lunch for everyone,* he thought to himself. Picking up the bucket, inhaling deeply the fresh clean air, he turned and walked back to the house without a second thought.

Chapter 8

Joseph ambled out of the conservancy across a small field of deep grass and headed back through the gate to his own property. He started to close the gate when suddenly he hesitated. He heard the cry again; this time it was close, and it wasn't the sound of pain. It was the deep growl of anger.

Joseph froze at the gate for a brief time, straining his eyes and ears to see or hear something that would give him a clue as to the source of the odd sounds, but nothing. He stayed a little longer, but all was silent save for the birds still happily fishing in the river. He decided it was just his imagination, locked the gate and continued the walk back to the house.

About halfway to the back door, something hit him hard in the back of the head. He whirled around to find no one there. Confused, he slowly turned a full circle, but could not find anything that could have caused such a blow.

Shrugging his shoulders, he took one step forward and his head exploded in extreme pain. For a moment he was frozen to the spot. Joseph couldn't move. His hands were stiff at his side; his feet were stuck, as if planted three feet into the soil. He could see and hear perfectly fine, but his body was not under his control. He was scared, really scared. He was sure he was having a stroke.

Somewhere from deep inside his head, Joseph, still rooted to the spot, heard a dark voice say, "I am Shingas. You shall pay. Vengeance is mine."

His body moved forward, but Joseph was not in control of it. He was in the grip of what could only be described as walking paralysis. He could see and hear everything, but he had absolutely no control over his body. He tried to scream, to call Katherine, anyone, for help, but his mouth was sealed shut as if his jaw were wired closed. He was a terrified prisoner in his own body.

He continued to move, rather his body continued to move, forward toward the house. As he walked through the yard toward the back door, he passed a tool he'd left on the ground. Stopping just long enough to stoop down, he saw his hand, not under his control, reach down and pick it up. He held it up and looked at it as if for the first time. His mind, in a state of horror, saw that he picked up a sickle that he had been using on some brush he was clearing out. It was sharp, smooth, and long with a curved end, perfect for slicing through thick brush. The voice in his head repeated, "I am Shingas. You shall pay." He once again stepped forward toward the house where his pregnant wife and beautiful son awaited his return. If he knew what was going to happen next, he would have slit his own throat; that is if his body would obey him.

Chapter 9

The fire department arrived within minutes of the 911 call. One of the neighbors was out walking his dog when he noticed the fire. There was smoke billowing from behind the house on Halstead. He quickly called 911, reported the fire, and just as quickly walked away from the scene. In New Jersey, the rule was not to get involved. If there was a fire, he did his civic duty. If there wasn't, then he wasn't going to stick around to be blamed for butting his nose into someone else's business.

The fire truck pulled up to the front of the house. Five firemen jumped off the truck. Two began to pull out hoses while two more headed around to the side of the house to see if they could ascertain what was burning. One went to the front door to see if anyone was home.

The two who went to the side of the house investigated the backyard and deduced that the barbecue was on its side and burning out of control. Somehow it had gotten knocked over, and the gas connection was ablaze. They hurried back to the truck to report what they saw and to get the gas wrench to shut off the valve.

"This should take only a minute to put out," Fireman Scott called to the others. "We can shut off the gas, knock it down with the extinguisher, and be back to the barn in half an hour." It was only partially true.

Scott grabbed the wrench and a fire extinguisher from the truck and headed to the backyard. Calling over his shoulder to the rest of the crew, he shouted, "I'll put this out. You guys wrap the hose back on the truck. There's no need for water."

"Okay," came the reply.

Scott lugged the extinguisher to the side of the house. He hopped over the split rail fence and found the gas valve located behind a small Japanese Boxwood that was planted to cover the valve from view. Most of the houses here had installed a gas line for their barbecues with a safety shut off on the back of the house, just in case of fire. Scott shut the valve with the wrench, knocked down the fire, and waited a minute to see if there were any embers that might reignite the blaze. He never looked up from the fire until it was out cold. Finally, he surveyed the scene, and nearly vomited on himself.

Chapter 10

The call came into the station precisely at 1:15 p.m. July 4th over the inter services radio system. Just after 9/11, New Jersey's governor outfitted the fire and police departments with an inter-agency radio communication system to prevent the miscommunication that caused so much controversy that fatal day back in 2001. Now if an emergency call came in over either system, the other department was able to monitor and respond immediately. Over the ensuing years this new system saved countless lives and assured prompt response by the proper emergency units.

Detectives Mercuri and Delair got the call and headed out. They pulled up to the scene and it was chaos. There were patrol cars, firetrucks, and neighbors all over the street. Paul looked at Dave and just shook his head in exasperation.

"Nothing like a shit storm to bring out the neighbors," he said as he and Dave headed to the firetruck to talk to the firemen.

"Yup."

Dave stood to the side and let Paul take the lead. "Can somebody tell me what happened here?"

"Well, that guy puking over there went around the back, put out the fire, and started screaming and tossing his cookies all over the yard," offered Fireman Alex, as he pointed to Scott who was slumped over the side of the fire truck.

Scott was drained of all color. One hand on the truck to steady himself, with the other hand holding his stomach, he continued to wretch. After a few more productive convulsions, it seemed his stomach was empty and now was only able to produce dry heaves. Scott looked at the officers heading his way, feared the questions he was sure was coming, rolled his eyes and began to heave all over again.

Scott was obviously in no condition to answer any questions, so Dave and Paul proceeded to walk around the side of the house and into the backyard. They reached the fence and surveyed the scene.

From what they could see from this vantage point, there was indeed a fire. The barbecue was tossed on its side, the ground was obviously burned, and there was some wood or something under the ruined barbecue. Upon closer examination, it wasn't wood. The rest of the yard was well laid out, neatly trimmed and well landscaped.

There were no immediate signs of a struggle or any intruder. Save for the burnt area around the barbecue, everything else looked normal. The detectives decided it was time for a closer inspection of the scene.

Dave looked at Paul and motioned, you first, as the two hopped the fence and headed toward the fire.

Carefully, trying not to disturb the area, Paul gasped as he kicked at the burned and charred "wood" that was on the ground. It wasn't wood. It was a pair of legs. Someone had been under the barbecue when it burst into flames. The natural gas fuel provided an intense inferno, which burned the body beyond recognition. Paul couldn't even tell if it was male or female, adult or child. Forensics would absolutely need to determine who this poor person was.

Dave saw something a little further in the backyard near a large chestnut tree. He decided to move closer to investigate. As he got closer, he wished he hadn't decided to look. There, upright against the tree, was the body of what appeared to be a young woman. She was naked, and split open from the base of the throat, down the centerline of her body, all the way to her crotch. What made it horrible beyond belief was the fact there was no blood. Her entrails were pulled out of her body and laid in a neat pile at her feet.

Puzzled by such a grotesque presentation, combined with the fact there was no blood anywhere, Dave continued to walk around the tree to see the precise spot where the brutal murder was committed. There was no blood on the ground around the tree; there was no blood on the tree and there was no blood anywhere on the body save for a few small droplets on the collar of the deceased blouse.

"How can there be this much bodily fluids and such extensive damage to the body, yet show no signs of blood anywhere at the scene?" Dave muttered, concluding that the woman was murdered elsewhere, and her body dumped there and put on display. If he wanted to find the murder scene, he knew he had to look elsewhere.

Turning away from the sight, Dave almost choked on his own vomit when he nearly stepped on something in the grass. It was slimy, red, and smelled awful. Trying not to upchuck, he coughed back his bile as he got a closer look. As soon as he did, he had to turn away as a plume of vomit exploded from his mouth. There, lying on the ground, was what looked like a mass of wet jelly about three feet across. There was a mass of something in the middle, like a glob of some kind swimming in the mass of fluids surrounding the contaminated area. Dave found the body of what could only have been an unborn baby girl.

It took Dave a few minutes to gather his thoughts. He and Paul sealed the crime scene, blocked off the area so no one could get a look, or worse yet, a photo of the gruesome tableau. People were shouting questions, which the detectives ignored. They headed back to the car to call it in. It was going to be a long day. It appeared they had a serial killer in the area and, whoever it was, was stepping up their game.

Chapter 11

In less than half an hour, the scene was crawling with CSI teams. Paul looked at Dave, who was still a little nauseous, and said, "They look like a colony of ants running all over the place."

Soon, one of the "ants" called over, "Detectives, you'd better come here and have a look at this," pointing to what appeared to be a hole in the ground.

The detectives reluctantly moved toward the tech, not wanting to see what he'd found, but knowing they had to look. They moved slowly with much effort as if to delay the inevitable. Unfortunately, they did arrive at the hole and Dave was forced to ask the inevitable question, "What've you got?"

The tech shook his head, and without saying a word, just pointed down at the hole. Dave was rooted to the spot, so Paul stepped forward. He soon wished he hadn't.

Peering over the hole, Paul audibly gasped, "Dear God," and stepped away from the horror within.

Lying there, at the base of the hole, about two feet down into the dark earth, lay the body of a young boy. He had been brutally butchered. Both his arms and his legs had been neatly sliced from his tiny body. Worst of all, his head was missing. Most confoundedly, there was no blood. How could something like this happen and who the hell would do such a thing?

Chapter 12

It was three days later that the call from the coroner's office came into the precinct. Dave took the call.

"This is Detective Delair," he said as he answered the phone."

"Hello, detective. This is Dr. Howell from the Middlesex County Coroner's office," replied Dr. Elizabeth Howell, Assistant Chief Medical Examiner for the county. "I am working on the Westons Mills case and I am afraid we have some, shall we say, unusual findings. I think you need to come down and see this."

"Whadda you got?" Dave asked with his New Jersey drawl in evidence.

"I really think you need to see this before I complete my report and it goes public," came the professional voice. "I think you need to come over now." This last part was more like an order rather than a request.

"Okay, be right there," replied Detective Delair with an obvious note of hesitancy in his voice. He really didn't want to see anything "unusual" This whole damn case was unusual. Bodies butchered, arms and legs cut off, no blood. What else could possibly happen? It was well beyond anyone's wildest imagination.

" What's up? "asked Paul as Dave hung up the phone.

"That was the coroner's office. Some doctor wants us to come on down to the cut shop and see something unusual."

"What could be more unusual than we have already? Bodies butchered, limbs missing and no blood?"

"Only one way to find out," Dave called over his shoulder as he headed out the door.

Dave reluctantly got behind the wheel as Paul jumped into the co-pilot seat. Dave let out a deep breath as he started the car and headed north on Kilpatrick street.

"Hey, isn't the coroner's office south?"

"Oh, yeah, that's right," replied Dave, in a monotone voice most unlike himself, as he continued to head in the wrong direction. It was as if someone else were driving. After twenty minutes of driving in circles, Dave finally steered the vehicle into the parking lot at 25 Kirkpatrick Street. They pulled up to the lot and hesitated before they opened the car doors and steeled themselves for whatever was going to happen next. The coroner's office loomed over them, foreboding, as they left their car in the "police only" parking area and headed toward the front entrance.

The Middlesex County Medical Examiner office consisted of a large governmental complex of buildings servicing the more than eight hundred thousand residents of the county. Here they provided services for the living, as well as the dead. The facility was designed to deal with highly complex and emotional issues, questions of law and religion and the interface between scientific technology and human variables. The facility was always busy, very busy.
Walking up the front steps into the medicinal smelling reception room, both detectives took in a deep breath and let

it out slowly. Paul walked up to the receptionist's window and said, "I am Detective Mercuri. That's my partner Detective Delair. We are here to see Dr. Howell."

Before the receptionist could respond, in walked a beautiful, lithe, thirty-something woman dressed in surgical scrubs covered by a pristine white lab coat. She stepped up to the detectives, introduced herself as Dr. Elizabeth Howell, shook their hands, spun on her heels, and commanded, "Follow me, please."

This one's all business, Paul thought and motioned to Dave with a shrug.

Following Dr. Howell, they passed through the realm of the living where there were scores of people waiting for various medical services from simple examinations to more complicated personal and mental issues. The building was teeming with life, while the detectives were here to deal with death.

They continued down several hallways, turning right and left, down two flights of stairs into the bowels of the building all while following a silent Dr. Howell. She didn't even look over her shoulder once to see if they were still behind her.

They finally reached the morgue area where the odor changed from medicinal to the acrid smell of death. They continued down the white tiled hall, past several examination rooms where all sorts of bodies were on display in various states of postmortem examination. The place gave Dave the willies; Paul was not too fond either, so both kept their eyes straight ahead, which provided a nice view of the doctor's form.

"This way detectives," said Dr. Howell, pushing a button on the wall, which engaged the automatic doors.

"You will need to put on lab coats, hair covering and booties to prevent any contamination of the evidence. This way please."

They entered a side chamber where, hung on the wall, were various sizes of lab coats, hats and a box of booties to cover their shoes. They each donned a lab coat, covered their shoes, and entered the exam room.

The room was covered from floor to ceiling with white tile, which made it easy to keep the suite clean. The room was lit, almost painfully lit, by several large surgical lamps that hung over each of five stainless steel examination tables. On each of the tables was something covered by a white sheet. Paul swallowed hard, trying not to get too nervous as he began to imagine what horrors were covered by the unassuming sheet. Dave just looked horrified.

"Detectives," began Dr. Howell, "as I mentioned over the phone, this case presented us with some very unusual findings. Follow me, please," she said as she headed toward the first table.

Whipping the sheet off with fanfare, Dr. Howell revealed the first horror. "Here we have the charred remains of an unknown adult. Tests showed the victim to be a male, age somewhere in the early thirties, identity unknown. The body was too destroyed by the fire to give a positive identification. We are still waiting on dental records."

The detectives were aghast at the condition of the body.

Without so much as a hesitation, the good doctor continued, "Judging from the condition of the body and the lack of any bodily fluids, I suggest the victim was burned alive and succumbed to his injuries within five minutes of the conflagration."

The doctor pointed to the victim's right hand. "Here we have what is most probably the murder weapon for the remaining victims. A common sickle, found in any good lawn and garden supply store. There was some blood on the handle that matched the female. It was certainly sharp enough to do the job, but there was a complication."

"Complication?" queried Paul. "What do you mean *complication*," he pressed, making imaginary quote marks in the air.

"Follow me."

They walked over to the second table and, again with a flourish most unnecessary (you could tell the doctor was enjoying this), revealed the second horror.

"Here we have the body of a gravid female of about thirty-something years of age. The body is split open from stem to stern. The entrails were surgically removed and a female fetus of approximately twenty weeks was removed and placed in a separate position from the entrails as described in the CSI report. There was no blood at the scene."

"That is a complication," remarked Dave.

Dr. Howell gave a disapproving glance at the detective, who promptly stifled another comment as the doctor continued. "The complication is not the lack of blood, although that in itself is interesting. It is the condition of the wound that is confusing. If you look closely…" The detectives did everything possible not to look closely, "…you can see that the incision was made from the inside out, as if something inside the body cut itself out rather than someone cutting in." Dr. Howell pulled open the incision, pointing at the flesh. "See here, the skin is cut smooth, but the adipose tissue under the skin is torn as you would expect from a cut made from the inside out. Very strange," she said, more to herself rather than for the benefit of the detectives. She repeated, "Very strange."

Breaking her out of her reverie, Paul asked, "How can that be? There is no way the cut could have come from the inside out."

"Detective, that is for you to figure out. I can only assure you that, based on detailed examination of the wound, the marks left on the sickle, and the overall condition of the body, it is evident that the incision was made from the inside out."

"Impossible."

"Maybe so, but the evidence proves otherwise. Now, over here, please," Dr. Howell moved over to a table holding remains obviously much smaller than the other two tables.

Unlike the previous reveals, Dr. Howell removed this sheet with reverence for the body beneath. Carefully, she drew back the cover to reveal the headless body of a young male child. The arms and legs had been surgically removed from the body and lay in proper orientation as if a model waiting to be assembled.

"Here we have the remains of a male child, approximately two years of age. Cause of death was most likely due to beheading, followed by desecration of the corpse by removal of the arms and legs. The head has not been recovered," was her matter of fact report.

'Who the hell could do this to a pregnant woman and a child?"

"That, detectives, is for you to find out. Next, we have the unborn fetus," intoned the doctor as she headed toward the final table cover.

Before she could remove the sheet, Dave spoke up. "Enough! I think we've seen enough. We don't need to see any more." It was he who found the fetus in the first place.

"Enough," he said again as he yanked off his lab coat, tore off his booties, and tossed them on the floor as he beat a hasty exit from the chamber of horrors.
Turning to the doctor, Paul said, "Thank you, doctor. We will be in touch if we need anything else."

As he turned to leave, the doctor spoke up for the final time. "Detective, you get that son of a bitch and make him pay for this."

"Yes, ma' am. We will."

Paul walked out into the hall to find Dave just pacing up and down. Knowing his partner very well, he decided to give him some space and let him come around.

After a few trips up and down the hall, Dave appeared to calm down a bit. Rubbing his hands through his hair, he looked Paul right in the eyes and declared, "What the hell kind of a perp can do this?"

"I have no idea," came the honest reply

"No blood. No evidence. No footprints, fibers, fingerprints. Nothing!" Dave shouted, working himself up all over again. Another trip up and down the hall. Scratching his face with a nervous gesture, Dave said, "Is this guy a ghost or something?"

Dave had no idea how close he was to the truth.

Chapter 13

The next few weeks were rife with bitter disappointment for the beleaguered detectives. Long hours spent following up dead-end leads, and no hard evidence coming forth, despite their herculean efforts, only soured their dispositions.

It was just another day at police headquarters. Cops were coming and going, the phones sang out a never-ending cacophony of background noise, and perps of every kind were singing their innocence to anyone who happened by. Delair and Mercuri shared a corner of the detective's bullpen located on the second floor of the building. It was crowded, noisy, and smelled a little like day old coffee.

The detectives were exhausted. Neither had slept more than a few hours a night since the case opened. Dave spent most of his time reading the reports and going over evidence, such as it was. Paul canvassed the neighbors, employers, relatives anyone who could add even a shred of evidence. Despite their meticulous detective work, they had nothing to go on.

Dave was distraught. He sat at his desk running his hands through his hair, a habit especially active when at wits end.

"How many times can we go through this and still have nothing?" The frustration in his voice clearly coming through to his partner. "We have been through this a hundred times and not a single shred of evidence leading to any potential perps."

"Let's go over it again, one more time. We have to have missed something," replied Paul running his hands, out of frustration and habit, through his dark Italian hair. "One more time. Okay?"

"Sure, why not? What the hell else we gonna do, right?" came the sarcastic response.

"That's the spirit"

"Piss off." Dave smiled for the first time in days.

"Okay, we have two crime scenes within blocks of each other," reported Paul as he began the litany of the known facts. "Four dead at each.

"Five at the first location, if we count the dog," added Dave.

With a snide, sideways grin, Paul corrected himself, "Eight people, one dog. Happy?"

Dave nodded in the affirmative without comment.

"First scene was covered in blood from the vics. Male vic was found with a knife presumably used to carve up his family, except for the wife, she died of a broken neck. At the second scene there was no blood from the vics, no sign of break-in, a sickle was confirmed as the murder weapon, found in the hands of the adult male vic. The male was also burned to ashes."

"That bothers me," interrupted Dave. "Why does a young guy kill his family out of nowhere then kill himself. No note, no sign of family hardship, everything to look forward to. New baby on the way. Makes no sense."

Just then the phone rang. "Saved by the bell," Paul chided as he picked up the receiver. "Detective Mercuri."

"Detective, this is Dr. Howell from the ME's office, I have some interesting information on the Westons Mills murder case."

Paul perked up. Finally, a lead. "Yes, Dr. Howell," he repeated for Dave's sake. "What evidence do you have for me?"

"I didn't say evidence, detective," she sounded like a teacher scolding a school boy. "I said I have some interesting information."

"Sorry, go on."

"Dental records confirmed the male to be the homeowner, a Dr. Joseph Farinola," she replied, shuffling a few papers. "The interesting point is that he was most likely dead before the fire."

Paul bolted upright in his chair. This caused Dave to startle and pepper Paul with questions, "What? What did she say? Come on man, what?"

Waving him off, Paul continued, "What do you mean the male was dead before the fire?" he repeated for Dave's benefit again.

Dave jumped up from his chair excitedly. Finally, something to hang their collective hats on.

"When I was taking x-rays of the jaw for the dental identification, I also shot the skull to see if there was any perimortem or postmortem damage evident. I found something that initially appeared to be the result of a severe blow to the head caused by a blunt instrument. It appeared that the blow fractured the frontal and lacrimal bones, which could have resulted in death or, at the very least, unconsciousness. Upon further examination, I found a small fragment not affiliated with the bone tissue. I removed the fragment and examined it to determine its origin."

"Yes, what was it?" Paul asked. He too jumped out of his seat and was walking in excited circles as far as the phone cord would allow. "What did you find?"

Letting out a deep breath, Dr. Howell replied, "The fragment appears to be animal bone."

"Animal bone? Where would that come from?"

"Precisely. I asked the same question myself. So, I did some research and determined it was actually from a white-tailed deer antler, the kind Native American Indians used to make battle axes or tomahawks. Upon further examination, the fragment appears to be old, maybe two hundred years or more. That's all I can tell you for now. I will keep digging."

Before Paul could quiz Dr. Howell further or even say thanks, she hung up.

Paul held the phone in his hands staring at the receiver, as if willing it to give more details. The phone remained silent. Paul returned the receiver to its cradle and sat down.

Dave was beside himself. "What did she say?"

"You're not going to believe this, but the second male was killed by an Indian tomahawk."

"Right, and I'm Sitting Bull."

"Well, you may or may not be Sitting Bull, but the good doctor seems to believe our vic was dispatched before he was burned, and the weapon was a deer antler that was more than two hundred years old."

Both detectives slumped further into their respective chairs and sat in stunned silence.

After a few minutes Dave spoke up, "Well, unless we can find some two-hundred-year-old Indian Chief, we are in no better place than before Dr. Howell called." "Well, at least we have a suspect," Paul said in jest as he tossed his report notes on the desk. "We better start looking for one pissed off Indian."

He had no idea how right he was.

Chapter 14

As for me, it was just another beautiful summer day in New Brunswick. I woke up before five a.m., as is my custom, headed out for my morning five-mile run and was back at the house by six. After my run, I treated myself to a hot shower, fixed a healthy breakfast of poached eggs and multigrain toast with peanut butter. I was now ready to start my day. I headed to the sun room to enjoy the newspaper.

The New Jersey Dispatch, the local news rag in the area, was awash with news about the murders. Well, news is not exactly correct. It was more speculation, sensationalism and morbid curiosity. The police had no clues and no suspects in the violent homicides. The paper focused on the ineptitude of the two local detectives, Paul Mercuri and Dave Delair, for their inability to close such a heinous case. They gave the detectives no quarter. It was brutal.

This was indeed a horror, not one I usually invested any time in, but it really hit a little too close to home for me. As a professor of biology at Cook College, Rutgers University, it was one of my colleagues, Dr. Joseph Farinola that was a victim of this brutal crime. Although I did not know him personally, I did recall meeting him at a faculty event last year. He seemed a nice fellow, very good looking and extremely intelligent, although he was not pretentious in the least. In fact, he was very down to earth. He had a great dry sense of humor that I really appreciated. It was a shame that his entire family was subjected to such a brutal murder. I truly hoped whoever was to blame would soon be caught and given the full punishments afforded by law. Privately, I thought they should cut his balls off first.

Although dismayed to read about murders so close to home, there was nothing I could do, so I finished paging through the rest of the news feed as I finished my third cup of java. Standing up from the sun room table, I headed into the kitchen where I dropped the coffee cup in the sink for later washing, tossed the paper in the recycle bin on my way to the hallway, and prepared to tackle the day's challenges.

Normally, I had to deal with the general mundane issues of academic life: the concerns of graduate students hoping to curry favor as they progressed in their studies. The occasional technical issues with my research on Avian Infectious Bronchitis Virus, would also sometimes present a challenge. I was working to complete the final phase of vaccine development. It could be tricky, but I had some brilliant graduate students on my team, so we usually could muddle through.

I still had much to prepare for the upcoming semester. Although I had been teaching the same subject for some years now, I always wanted to include new findings in the field and consistently tried to improve the core content to try to reach as many students as possible. This was sometimes a daunting task.

Infrequently, thank God, I had to deal with the politics often seen at major universities. Who got tenure and who didn't was always at the forefront of the discussions. Thankfully, I was tenured, so I stayed as far away from these political bombs as possible. Today, however, would present with challenges well beyond my meager capabilities.

I headed out of the house at 22 Seaman Street and was greeted by a beautiful August day. There were only three weeks of summer vacation left after which another crop of young wide eyed, innocent students would invade our sanctum of higher education. The sun was shining brightly; its rays played peek-a-boo through the leaves of the stately trees that lined both sides of the street of this residential community. My home was only one block off the immense campuses of the combined Douglas College and Cook College both part of Rutgers, University. Each day I would turn west towards Nichol Avenue for the short walk to Thompson Hall, the location of my office and lab.

Today, for some reason, I veered off my habitual course on my way to the office. The morning was warm, and the air smelled so sweet that I wanted to take an extra moment to appreciate the weather. Fall was not always kind in New Jersey, so I wanted to enjoy this summer day before it was gone. So, instead of heading for the stuffy environs of my 150-year-old basement lab in Thompson Hall, I headed across the lawn behind the greenhouses and crossed Red Oak Road over to an old wooden bench near the corner of Red Oak Road and Lipman Drive.

The old bench had occupied this spot for as long as I could remember. It was of wooden construction; two by fours bolted to a metal frame comprised the simple structure. The bench was coated with layers upon layers of paint, building up over the years to hide its true age. Much like me.

The surface of the bench was covered with initials of students, lovers, and friends carved, some deeply, into the wood, while others only marred the paint. Perhaps a sign of what was deep and long lived versus that which is shallow and possibly fleeting. This bench, if it could talk, had many stories to tell. I had my own stories on this bench. Thank God, it was silent.

I have many fond memories of this spot. There was a time during my very long life I spent many a day walking by this bench on my way to the lab. I would sometimes see someone sitting here, enjoying the solitude and wish I could stop and talk, but my condition at the time did not allow. There were, however, certain circumstances that would allow my interaction.

My fondest memory was my last at the bench. It was here a very, very long time ago I met Cathy. She was a young psychology student at Douglass College. She was beautiful, smart, and blind. She and I would meet here almost daily over the course of several months. I felt safe with her. That was until she tried to "help me move on" as she put it. I was not ready to "move on" then and I am not ready now. Although my circumstances today are far different from that time, I still recall with sadness how things ended. I wished things could have lasted longer, but they didn't.

As I was sitting in my reverie, lost in memories of things past, I suddenly felt a chill as if "someone walked over my grave," as my mother would have said.

I felt such an uncomfortable chill up and down my spine that I jumped up from the bench. My hackles were up, my arms were replete with goosebumps, and my heart was racing, as if I had just run a mile. I had no idea what was going on. I thought I was prepared for anything. But I was not prepared for him.

Chapter 15

"Good morning, Dr. Mauro."

I was in shock. There before my eyes stood a man I had not seen in nearly two decades, and he was greeting me like we last spoke only yesterday. Every muscle in my body was taut. I was not a man prone to violence, but I felt my hands, beyond my control, clenched in fists of rage. It took all my willpower to force them to relax and remain safely at my sides.

We stood there staring at each other in silence. He was elegantly dressed as always. Standing over six foot two, his hair was jet-black and perfectly coiffed. His suit was impeccable, an Armani I presumed. It was perfectly tailored to hang handsomely no matter what position he assumed. His white starched shirt did not bear even the hint of a wrinkle. The outfit was complete with a subdued red tie, tied in a complicated full Edwardian knot. Of course, he smelled of rose petals, a scent which befitted his nature.

We continued to stand toe to toe in silence. I had no voice with which to speak. I was angry, hurt, and shocked to see him standing there looking exactly as he was the last time I saw him walking away from me at the hospital. Finally, I screwed up the courage to speak.

"Is that the best you can do after all this time? *Good morning, Dr. Mauro.*" My face was flushed with emotion, anger being the most prevalent. We stood there on the sidewalk, eye to eye without blinking, each taking the measure of the other.

Finally, I lashed out. "You abandoned when I needed you most. First you send me, alone, across time and space to fight the embodiment of evil himself!" My voice was high and shrill, declaring my highly charged emotional state. "I returned through a portal of your making, nearly dead from the ordeal and you disappear! I needed you then, where were you? Gone!" I shouted, stepping one step closer on the verge of hysteria.

"Where were you then? I needed you, and you were gone," I repeated sounding more hurt than angry. Looking away from him toward the ground at my feet, I tried to control myself, but I felt the anger rising again. "Now, you have the audacity to stand before me as if nothing has happened, how dare you!" I was breathing hard, sweat rolled down my forehead as my heart beat to the tempo of a rock band drummer. "You come here, to this time and place and bid me good morning." I shook my head as if to show both disbelief and disapproval at his return.

Patiently, taking my abuse, he stood there a moment longer. He was calm as always. After what seemed to be an eternity, he opened his mouth to speak and offered, "I am sure you have many questions, we will have time enough for that, but I come to you once again in need."

I was stunned silent again. My emotions were running the gamut. I wanted to yell. I wanted to scream expletives. I wanted to demand he answer my questions right now. He had abandoned me those many years ago, abandoned me right after he sent me on a quest that he himself felt would spell my doom. He walked out on me just when I needed him the most. He left me alone all these years. The anger was

70

building up all over again. Before I could say anything, he said in his most unassuming tone, "I never abandoned you. I was always with you. I know you have questions, and I said I will answer them, one and all. But, for now, I need your assistance once again."

I felt the angry emotions in my body begin to ebb. Just hearing his voice, the lilt of his tone, the sincere look on his angelic face calmed my senses. I felt at once, calm. With my emotions checked, I looked at him and asked, "Why?"

For a moment I could see what looked like sorrow cross his brow. I could see in his visage that he felt concern and something akin to love for me. He sighed, brushed his right hand through his hair, a habit of his, and spoke in that soothing tone once again. "Robbie, there is much to know and much that cannot be known. Suffice it to say you were not, nor will you ever be, alone. I have been and shall be with you always. All is not as it seems. I need you now for another quest."

I stood there aghast. "Another quest?" The last time I went on his "quest" I suffered unknown horrors.

As if reading my mind, he conceded, "It is true that the last time we met you did indeed suffer hardship, but in the end, you got your life back. Did you not?"

"Yes," was all I could say just above a whisper.

"Good, I ask only that you hear me out. I will tell you what you need to know, and you can make your own decision. But let me tell you this, the lives of many innocent people hang on

71

your decision. You can prevent additional suffering, or you can turn your back and leave once we have finished. The choice remains yours and yours alone."

I was intrigued. I could not reply, so I nodded slightly, showing my assent to his request.

"Good then. Meet me at Tabor house..."

Before he could complete his thought, I cut him off, "Precisely at midnight?"

He cocked his head and raised an eyebrow in a move reminiscent of one Mr. Spoke and continued, "I see you have not forgotten." He smiled, then, without waiting for further comment or question, he bowed slightly, as would a fine English gentleman, turned swiftly on his heels and walked away. I watched, rooted to the spot, as he gracefully walked out of view. For a moment I thought, "Did that just happen?"

Yes, indeed that did just happen, as would so much more.

Chapter 16

I remained frozen to the spot shaking from head to toe. I could feel the burst of adrenaline coursing through my body. I felt my hands clench in a tight fist, and then relax for a moment only to clench once again. I was angry, hurt, perplexed, and more than a little scared all at once. My heart was beating so hard I thought I would pass out. I was sweating so profusely that I had to wipe my eyes as salty sweat dripped from by brow.

"This was not how I planned to begin this day," I whined out loud to myself. *Now he has me talking to myself again*, I thought, this time keeping the words inside my head. *What next?*

I stood on the sidewalk in front of Thompson Hall debating with myself what I should do next. I turned toward the entrance to my basement lab and stopped before I even crossed the sidewalk. There was no way I was going to do any work today, still clenching and unclenching my fists. *Go home*, said the voice in my head.

I stood for another moment considering again what just happened. I had not seen Ezerial for nearly two decades and he just popped in as if nothing happened. The last time I saw him much happened. In fact, everything that I once was and all that I became was because of Ezerial and our first meeting. And just like that he had popped back in and told me he needed my help again.

On the one hand, I was fuming. On the other hand, I was indebted to Ezerial; after all it was he who had given me my life back. This life I have lived for the last nearly twenty years.

Although I could not explain it, I did owe him something. The least I could do was listen to what he had to say. I owed him at least that much, right? Again, I was arguing with the voice in my head.

Taking in a deep breath and letting it out slowly, hoping to calm my raging emotions, I turned from the path leading to my lab and headed back out to Nichol Avenue. As I reached the corner, I was tempted to turn left toward Tabor House rather than right toward my home on Seaman Street. But I knew it would be of no use.

"Meet me precisely at midnight as before," Ezerial admonished before leaving. The last time I went looking for him at Tabor House, the residence he supposedly shared with the University minister, I was surprised to say the least.

As I recall on the day I left the hospital I was given the gift of a new life: a home on Seaman Street, compliments of the University ministry, and a position of a professorship in the Department of Biology, all neatly arranged by the mysterious Ezerial. I was told in a letter from Ezerial these were my rewards for having helped him vanquish Azazel, the only son of Samyaza, an angry demon hell bent on destroying our world. Yeah, I didn't believe it either, but it really did happen, and I am living proof.

So, instead of confronting Ezerial, I reluctantly turned right and walked the several blocks to my home in silence. Even the voice in my head was quiet.

I bounded up the steps and headed into the foyer and walked through the entrance hall into the living room. I stopped by the right side of the ancient fireplace and reached under the lintel and popped a lever that opened a secret door to the right of the fireplace. I opened the door which revealed a narrow spiral staircase leading up to a hidden room where I once lived so long ago in my first life.

The room was as I left it, my grandmother's bentwood rocking chair still covered with her blanket. A pillow rested on the seat, another gift from my beloved grandmother. All around were memories of the past, the past I almost had forgotten these past 100 years.

I moved the pillow, sat on the rocker, and covered myself with the blanket, not for warmth but for comfort, knowing that the spirit of my long dead grandmother was still with me. I rocked and remembered.

I was born in the year 1893 in the Harlem section of what was then the Italian section of New York City. I grew up in a close-knit family and, shortly after my fifth birthday, the family moved to a duplex in the Gravesend section of Brooklyn.

How prophetic was the name Gravesend? It was here that my two best friends, Roger and Mark, and I grew up together, inseparable until the horrible events that tore us apart.

You see, we once found an ancient Ouija board, owned by the boys' Gypsy grandmother. Inevitably, we did the unthinkable and played with the board. Unfortunately, we opened the door to a place that ultimately cost me my life. I refused to be "dead" and so remained "in between" this world and the nothing that was the next.

It was in this state of non-being that I first came across Ezerial. He told me a fantastic story, one that I doubted then, but truly believe now.

Ezerial told me that he was a Watcher. He was one of the beings sent down eons ago to watch over mankind. They were commanded by the Almighty to observe and not interfere. Unfortunately, several of the Watchers chose to disobey the Supreme Being and, as a punishment, he sent down the Great Flood in the time of Noah and destroyed all of mankind, including the Watchers.

Unfortunately, one being, a hybrid, born of a Watcher and a mortal, survived the deluge and vowed to destroy the Almighty's creation.

Ezerial enlisted me to help him destroy the demon named Azazel and, in so doing, I was rewarded with a corporeal body and the chance to live my life again. I know it sounds impossible and, if it hadn't happened to me, I would be the first to say "Bullshit," but I swear to you every word is true.

I sat in my grandmother's chair all day and thought about the past, the trials that brought me to this very spot, and the request Ezerial put upon me to meet with him and hear his story. I knew I had no real choice but to obey.

It was growing late, so I fixed myself some dinner, had a drink or two to settle my nerves, and waited for the hours to pass. It was soon time to go. I left the comfort and safety of my grandmother's chair, folded the blanket and replaced the pillow just as they were earlier, and turned to head down the spiral staircase to face the future.

76

I stood at the top of the stairs, stopped, and slowly looked around the room. I spent many a peaceful time in this space. I wondered if I would ever see it again. Taking it all in, possibly for the last time, I breathed deeply the fragrance of my past and headed down the stairs, out into the future.

Chapter 17

It was about 11:30 at night when I left, locked the front door, and stood for a moment on the front porch gazing out into the sky. It was very bright for so late at night. I looked up to see a beautiful bright, white full moon. Of course, it would be a full moon. Shaking my head, I headed down the porch steps and onto the sidewalk.

There was a slight chill to the August evening; fall would soon be upon us. The air had the slight sweet fragrance of evening primrose. I stopped for a moment to take it all in. With a sigh that came from nowhere, I turned right, and started walking slowly toward my destination at Tabor House.

When I was a student here a very long time ago, I was first introduced to Tabor House as the residence of the local campus ministry. The original Tabor house, named after the biblical Mt Tabor, the site of the transfiguration of Christ, was originally built in 1869. There were several iterations and expansions over the years. The building still retained its colonial charm while providing a very welcoming atmosphere to all who crossed its threshold.

As I walked down Seaman Street, I turned right at the Nichols Avenue intersection and continued a few blocks to the wrought iron gate that surrounded the property, protecting yet welcoming at the same time.

I stood for a moment, my hand on the gate, contemplating whether to turn and run or go forth and face the challenges ahead. I was truly torn, but as I said before, I did owe Ezerial my life, such as it is. I convinced myself to at least listen to what he had to say, so I steeled myself against what was to come, sighed deeply once again, squared my shoulders, and soldiered forth toward the unknown.

On the front door of Tabor House was a hand carved wooden Chi Rho Christogram and a sign welcoming all to a house of God. It was nearly midnight, the appointed hour.

I knew from experience that the door would be unlocked. Half hoping it was locked, I reached out and turned the door knob. It opened easily. I winced as I entered the residence.

Now, one would expect that the home of a poor minister of Christ, and shepherd to a flock of college students would be living in very basic accommodations, perhaps even Spartan by local standards.

Such was not the case, however. Upon entering the hall, I could see that there were no lights in the house save for a small light in a room to my left. I had visited this room before and knew it as the library. I turned from the entry and made my way silently toward the light.

The last time I was in this room was twenty years ago, and at that time the room had two tired, old, upholstered chairs, a table with mismatched lamp, some small bookcases with a few magazines and copies of pamphlets normally reserved for stimulating discussions with the students who frequented the abode of the affable parish priest. On the floor was a worm- eaten rug that covered a wooden floor marred by deep scuffs and scratches from millions of steps taken across its surface over the years.

The sight before me on this night, precisely at midnight, was far grander. Covering the center of a highly polished wooden plank floor was a pristine hand woven oriental rug of exquisite design. The sloppy upholstered chairs were replaced with fine, red leather, high back Edwardian chairs, obviously antique and worth a fortune. The reading table held a single lamp, which cast a fine yellow glow about the room.

Lifting my eyes, I saw before me a series of hand- tooled walnut bookcases covering three of the four walls. The bookcases stood floor to ceiling and were filled to bursting with every type of rare book and manuscript imaginable.

There were books bound in carved leather, obviously of ancient vintage. Some books were as thick as three inches, probably Bibles from various ages. Each book was carefully placed by subject and reverently preserved as if they were of the utmost value to their owner, which of course they were.

As I marveled once again at the immensity and complexity of this library, I heard a voice to my right.

"Welcome," it proffered in a sound above a whisper.

I spun around, startled, as I had not heard anyone enter the room. There, sitting in one of the leather chairs, neatly dressed in his dark Armani Suit, starched white shirt, sedate red tie and blindingly polished leather wingtips, sat Ezerial.

"I am so glad you decided to accept my invitation."

Chapter 18

I stood as if planted to the spot, unable to move or reply. I could feel my guts turning, my body was trembling. I was angry, angry beyond words. I could feel my fists open and clench over and over. I wasn't even trying to remain calm. I began to sweat, not from the temperature in the room, but from the internal flames of anger. Before I could say a word, Ezerial looked me right in the eyes and, in a most calming tone, offered, "I know you are angry. You feel I left you. But as I have said before, all is not what it seems. I was always with you, you were never alone."

What happened next amazed me to the core. The anger, hot and deep, swept out of me like a cool breeze. I wanted to hold on to the anger; to yell, to scream, but instead I suddenly felt at peace. Calm. Soothed to the point where my entire being, both mental and physical, relaxed. I felt drained; unable to stand any longer, I limped over to the matching chair and fell into the soft leather. I was breathing hard, exhausted. My heart was pounding from shear stress, but I was no longer angry.

Why?

We sat in silence, each lost in our own thoughts. Ezerial pulled at the cuff of his suit, straightened the crease on his pants then assumed a pose so characteristic of our first meeting in this room.

Gently and ever so elegantly, he brought his hands together as if in prayer, then he folded over his thumbs, brought the index fingers under his chin and folded over the remaining fingers, a pose of deep contemplation. He sat motionless, looking at me; no through me, as if to ascertain my innermost thoughts. He made no sound. He allowed a single slight sigh to escape his lips as he waited for me to speak.

I remained in my chair and suddenly I felt relief, comfort, even warmth. My heart slowed to a normal rhythm. My breathing, once shallow and angry, was now deep and soothing. I felt the deep warmth of the leather chair surround me and was at peace. I, too, sighed and could only muster a single word, "Why?"

"Robbie," he began in a fatherly tone, "you were never alone. I was always with you, watching, guiding, and providing a source of comfort when you needed it most. I am forever grateful to you for what you have done at my behest. There was no one in existence who could do for me what you have done and for this you were rewarded with the return of your corporeal body, to finish a life cut far too short. But now we once again face an evil presence, for which I need your assistance to combat. You are under no obligation to help me, I would understand completely if you did not, but many lives will be lost if we do not intercede."

I was stunned silent. My mind was racing on so many fronts. I was never alone, he was always with me? How could that be? I was confused. He left me alone, without a word of goodbye, yet he tells me I was not alone. A look of confusion must have crossed my face for he continued, "You, of all men, understand that which is not known. You have experienced things that no man has or will ever experience, and yet you doubt me?"

His tone was not accusatory, but almost hurt, as if my doubts cut him deeply. Suddenly I was sorry for my thoughts. Then it hit me, these were my thoughts, I voiced no words. Ezerial could reach into the very depths of my mind. I knew then, he was right. I was never alone. That voice, that voice in my head, the one that from time to time gave direction when I was confused, could it really have been him?

I looked over and he just nodded as if answering the unasked question. After a moment, he cocked his head and asked, "May we continue? There is much to learn and precious little time to learn it."

I sat there, comfortably in the elegant leather chair, calm in both mind and body. I rubbed my hand on the arms of the chair, relishing the feel of the soft leather against my skin. Smiling, I looked directly at the Watcher and offered, "I am once again at your service."

For the first time in a very long time, I felt complete. He carefully adjusted his position in the chair, smiled in my direction and proclaimed, "Good, then return tomorrow at the appointed hour and we shall begin our quest."

And so, we began.

Chapter 19

This was not going to be a good day, Captain Capella thought as he crossed his expansive office, morning cup of joe in one hand, the local newspaper in the other. Plastered across the front page was the banner headline:

"Another Family Massacred; Police Clueless"

Captain Joseph Capella was a big man. Standing six feet five inches, his close cropped black hair and huge shoulders belied his Italian ancestry. From the day he could talk, he wanted to be a cop. His father was a cop and his grandfather before him was a cop. So, Joe was going to be a cop. Period.

Joe studied hard in school, got good grades and when he graduated high school he immediately applied to the Monmouth County Police Academy, a prestigious school where he excelled in all phases of police work. He didn't graduate number one, but he was in the top five and his parents were proud.

At the graduation party his father hoisted a glass of fine chianti and predicted to all, "Someday my boy will the Captain of the force.!" How prophetic that day was. Capella worked hard. First as a beat cop, then a detective working his way up to homicide where he earned his lieutenant stripes. After fifteen years working the street, Joe was promoted to the administrative side of the ledger where he continued his rise to the present position of Captain.

Although he had a force of over two-hundred under his command, he never forgot where he came from and what it was like on the streets. He defended his officers and gave them the latitude they needed to keep the people safe. He never interfered and, so, was well respected by his command. That could all change.

As Joe sat down behind his desk, always cluttered with papers, booking sheets, mugshots and the general squalor of society, Joe thought, *today was not going to be a good day to be a cop*. He was just bringing the coffee mug to his lips, when, suddenly the door flew open and a newspaper flew across the room landing smack in the middle of his desk. Joe almost spilled his coffee. Looking up, with a scowl darkening his face, he was not too surprised to see Mayor Burns storm into the room.

"What in the hell is going on, Capella?" the mayor shouted, his normal mode of communication. "Your force is making me look like an asshole."

Capella hated the mayor. Mayor Randolph Burns, Randy to his friends, because he was always randy, was not elected to the lofty position of New Brunswick Mayor. Instead he orchestrated the demise of the duly elected Mayor, Pat Sheehan, by spreading lies, innuendo, and false evidence until the mayor was forced to resign and Randy was appointed the new head of New Brunswick. Nothing was beneath Randy. He was all for himself and would happily throw his grandmother under a bus if he could look better doing it.

"Good morning to you as well, sir," offered Captain Capella, knowing it would set the mayor off again.

85

"Good morning?" shouted Burns. "Drop dead, asshole. Can't you read? The headline in today's paper is unacceptable. It makes me look like a fool, running a city that allows murders to happen to my citizens and I can't do anything about it. What the hell are you doing to fix this?" Burns continued the tirade at the top of his lungs.

"We are working diligently, following up every lead and working the case." Capella responded with platitudes, designed to piss the mayor off even more.

"Leads!" he shouted. "It says right here you have no leads. In fact, you are completely lost. What the hell are you doing to me? This is an election year. I was elected"

Capella interrupted, "Sir, you were appointed, not elected." Capella loved to throw fuel on the already burning mayor.

"Shut up, Capella. If you can't find this guy, and find him soon, we'll see how long it takes you to find another job!" The mayor stormed out, slamming the door behind him for emphasis.

"Good riddance to bad news," Capella said out loud. Reaching over to the phone on his desk, he pressed the intercom and connected to Connie Polk his secretary.

"Connie, can you please tell Detectives Mercuri and Delair to join me in my office."

"Would this have anything to do with the condition of the mayor? "Connie chided.

"Indeed, it does."

"Right away, Captain"

"Thanks, Connie." The captain passed his hand across his face, as if to wipe off the grime left from his conversation with the mayor.

A moment later, Paul and Dave entered the office. Dave came in first, followed by Paul, who instinctively closed the door.

"Morning, Captain. You wanted to see us?" queried Dave.

Without preamble, the captain pointed to the two chairs in front of his desk. "Sit." The detectives complied, looking like two school boys who had just been called into the principal's office. "I am sure you saw his horror coming out of my office this morning."

"Saw and heard, sir." replied Paul.

"Then I guess you know he's none too pleased with the progress on this case. He wants answers and he wants them yesterday."

"Yes, sir," came the joint reply.

"Look, I know you two are working hard on this case. I was in your shoes once myself. I can block and dodge the turd as best as I can, but we need progress and we need it pronto, capiche?"

"Yes, sir."

"Okay, then get the hell out of my office, get me something, anything that moves this along, and no more newspaper stories," Captain Capella said, smiling as he admonished the detectives.

"Thank you, sir, for your support, we will not let you down," offered Dave, thankful that the captain was angrier at the mayor and not them.

"I know. Now get the hell outta here and ask Connie if she would please bring me another coffee, this cup was fouled by the mayor's presence." Dismissing his men, Captain Capella sat down and began to shuffle through the never-ending paperwork on his desk.

Paul and Dave thanked him once again and left the office, thankful they were still on the case and on the job. Some officers have been damned for less, much less.

Chapter 20

"Well, the rags got one thing right; we have no clues"

"You nerd, that's not what they mean. They are saying you and I are clueless," chided Detective Delair, as he tossed a pencil across his desk at his partner.

"Hey, I know." The younger detective ducked the well-aimed pencil. "I was just trying not to let them get to us. But, seriously, we have no clues except a fragment of bone that could be from a Tomahawk," Paul replied, shaking his head in disbelief at what he just said. "Now the murders are starting to look like the work of a single nutcase."

"Yeah, I know. Damn it." Delair ran his hands through his hair, a habit born out of frustration and exhaustion. "What do we have on the latest crime scene?"

Paul read from his report, "The residence at Agate Road in Westons Mills appeared to be secure, with no immediate sign of disturbance as we rode up to the scene. Detective Delair checked the front door while I headed toward the back of the house to check the back door. Upon entering the backyard, I came across four homicide victims. They were lined up in the middle of the back yard in a ceremonial or cult-like fashion, each holding hands. The three female victims were on their backs facing the sky. The male victim was also on his back but was facing the wife as if to look at her in death.

"Jesus," was all Delair could muster as the grisly scene played over in his head.

Paul continued, "I called my partner over the radio and we secured the area. The victims appeared to be husband and wife and two daughters, approximate age between ten and thirteen. The female, assumed to be the mother of the siblings, appeared at first glance to be asleep. Upon close inspection her hands, feet and head were severed from the body and placed on the ground in proper position to the body."

Delair interrupted again, "Who the hell could do something like that and leave nothing behind? "

Paul shrugged and continued reading, "The two young females were also savagely beaten and appeared to suffer stab wounds to the face, head and neck. Both victims were cut deeply across the neck, almost severing the head from the body."

Again, Delair interrupted, "With all that blood, with so much contact with the victims, there were no unidentified footprints, hair, blood, fibers nothing?" Throwing his hands out toward his partner, he exclaimed, "How can that possibly be? Unless this guy is some kind of ghost or attacks his victims covered in a Tyvek suit, he has to leave something behind."

"Or she."

"What?" said Dave.

"You said 'he.' It could very well be a 'she' since we have no clues as to the unsub's gender; we can't rule it out."

"She, *really*? Do you think a woman is really capable of doing such hideous damage to kids? She would have to be some high-on-the-hill wacko to do this kind of brutality."

"I'm just saying, until we have something more to go on we have to keep an open mind on all aspects of the case. Shall I continue?"

"Yeah go on."

"The male victim appeared to be covered in the blood of the other victims as his clothes were covered in blood spatter inconsistent with his wounds. This was confirmed upon forensic examination.

The male suffered severe trauma to the chest and appeared to have been cut open and his heart removed. No sign of the heart was found at the scene or in later investigation. The heart is still missing."

Paul put the report down and pushed back in his desk chair. He just sat there staring at the report as if it was going to jump off his desk.

Detective Delair finally broke the silence. "Who the hell could do such a thing?"

"From the outside, it almost looks cut and dry."

"How so?"

Paul gave voice to a theory he was working on. "Look the male is covered in blood of the other vics. Same in all the cases so far, right?"

"Go on."

"Okay, the father goes nuts, kills his family and then himself. It happens all the time, right?"

"Okay, smart guy, then tell me how the latest family is killed by the crazy father, then he cuts his own heart out and loses it."

"Yeah, well there's that."

"Yeah, well, there is that. Nice try, smart guy, but we are no further along in these cases and I am afraid we're going to see more before this is done."

The phone on Dave's desk rang. Neither reached for it, not wanting to hear that another family had been slaughtered.

Finally, after the tenth ring, Dave said, "Geesh," and reached to answer the call.

Putting the receiver to his ear, he never had time to say anything when a very excited female voice said, "Get over here right away. I found something." He didn't need to ask who it was.

Dave jumped up from his desk chair and called over to his partner, "Let's go, Bunko. The good Dr. Howell wants to treat us to another of her ghoul sessions."

"What?" Paul uttered.

"The good doctor found something she wishes to share with us lowly detectives. So, get your butt moving. We are heading over to the M.E.'s office for a tour of dead bodies."

When they arrived at the offices of the Medical Examiner, Dr. Howell had left instructions for the two detectives to head right down to the autopsy theater. They donned white coats, green hats and rubber gloves, put booties over their shoes and entered the domain of the beautiful but focused Dr. Elizabeth Howell.

"Detectives, this way." The order came from the far side of the room.

They crossed the room, which had been carefully arranged so that multiple autopsies could be carried out at the same time without interference from each table. It was a model of efficiency. Today, however, the theater was empty save for the four victims, the detectives and Dr. Howell.

"Over here, detectives, this is most unusual," called Dr. Howell, not bothering to lift her head from the autopsy table as she had her hands elbow deep in the viscera of the male victim. "This way, quickly. Fascinating," she whispered mostly to herself.

Approaching the table from the opposite side from where the good doctor was working, the detectives peered over the body while Dr. Howell continued.

"Look at this. You see that the heart was surgically removed from the male victim. Each major artery was severed individually and neatly and with some level of expertise. Based on the amount of clotted blood in the body cavity, I would venture to say the victim was alive and alert when the aorta was severed. This caused rapid exsanguination and swift death. The victim knew he was bleeding to death."

She paused before continuing. "The heart is the only organ missing from the body. The instrument used to remove the organ was extremely sharp but appears to have been other than a scalpel. See here, along this rib, there is a cut mark from a cutting instrument used to open the body so that the unsub could get to the heart for removal."

The detectives nodded without looking. The scene was disturbing enough, and Dave really didn't want to toss his cookies again.

As the doctor examined the bone marks closely, she exclaimed, unable to control her excitement, "Look, a fragment. Something is stuck in the back side of this rib bone. Gentlemen, we have our second piece of evidence." Howell looked up from the body for the first time, smiling.

My God, she is beautiful, thought Delair, before shaking the thought from his head. *Get back in the game, man.*

The doctor was back looking down into the body, then without looking up said, "Hand me those forceps."

The detectives looked at each other quizzically, shaking their heads in confusion. Dr. Howell snapped her fingers expectantly, while staring at inside the body. Paul shrugged and picked up an instrument and handed it to her.

"That's a hemostat, but it will do, "she retorted, taking the instrument from Paul's hands and digging around the back side of the third rib. After a moment, she jumped up from the body holding the instrument for all to see and proudly exclaimed, "Got it! Now what the hell is it?"

She turned the fragment over and over in her hands. She furrowed her forehead. "I have no idea what this is, but it does not belong in that body, so someone put it there. If we find out whom, then you will have your killer, detectives."

Without another word, she fled the autopsy theater and headed over to her lab for further examination under the microscope. The detectives headed to the locker room to change out of their protective clothing and await the doctor's findings. They didn't have long to wait.

By the time they had doffed their gear Dr. Howell came into the locker room with the fragment neatly contained in an evidence bag.

She handed it to Delair and said, "I have no idea how or why that fragment was in the victim's rib, but I can assure you it indeed was part of a cutting instrument that was conclusively used to open the victim's chest. From what I can gather, the unsub cut into the victim using a blade made of knapped flint. What you are holding is a fragment that broke off when the unsub hit the third rib while he was opening the victim to get to the heart."

"Knapped flint, what the hell is that?" queried Dave, as he examined the bag before handing it to Paul.

Howell put on her lecturing persona and replied, "Flint knapping is the age-old art of making arrowheads and other edged stone tools, such as knives and skinning instruments used by native American Indians. Hunter gatherers relied upon this key wilderness survival skill to create important tools and hunting implements. Many people continue to practice the skill today, including traditional bowyers, experimental archaeologists, and primitive skills enthusiasts. At its most basic level, flintknapping consists of breaking open a piece of parent material, called a core, striking flakes off that core, and then shaping those flakes into the intended tool."

The detectives stood there stunned at the revelation. But that was not the end of the report. "One more thing."

Simultaneously, both detectives asked, "What else?"

"Like the previous female victim, this person was cut from the inside out."

Chapter 21

The detectives needed to have a space where they could work the case undisturbed. It soon became evident that the shared quarters in the busy detective bullpen was not conducive to focused endeavors. The busy precinct, with the constant comings and goings of officers and perp's, the occasional "crazy person" in lock up, and the somewhat obtrusive chiding from the other detectives, continued to interrupt their efforts. Something had to change. So, they decided they needed more private quarters.

Thus the "War Room" was set up in the basement of Paul's mother, Phyllis' house located a few blocks away from his own apartment. The ever-doting Italian mother would do anything to spend more time with her beloved son, even if he has yet to produce a grandchild. Since hope springs eternal, Phyllis was all too eager to allow Paul unfettered access to the basement environs. After all it would allow her time to spend with her eldest son. She envisioned dropping in with snacks, homemade of course. She saw them sitting together and just having some mother/son time. That is until she went down stairs for the first time and got a good look at what was going on there. One look at the items on the whiteboards was enough to turn her stomach. As long as the detectives were downstairs working on that horrid case, she vowed never to go down those stairs again. And she didn't.

Paul had commandeered several clean white wall boards, which he fashioned into a modified cork board and whiteboard combination. The boards were strategically positioned so that a person sitting in the middle of the room had a perfect view of each board and what it contained. He had positioned lights, writing tables, chairs, all just so, allowing he and Dave access to every detail, photograph and evidence bag as they evaluated the clues, looking for something that held the pieces together.

The boards were labeled Crime Scene one through three. On each board he had the names of the victims, a description of the scene, multiple grisly photographs, and notes expressing ideas as to what happened and possible connections. Each board was almost filled to capacity with notes, diagrams, concepts written down then crossed out, rejected only to be replaced by other ideas that were soon equally rejected. The fourth board contained a list of facts the detectives believed were important points that could be clues, but none seemed to lead anywhere.

Paul had thought of everything. There was a refrigerator, a bathroom, even a cot in case one needed to lie down. The center cement floor was covered with a rubber mat to help alleviate leg strain as they paced back and forth from one board to the next, evaluating, contemplating and revising theories, hypotheses and just plain ideas. All for naught.

It was Dave who finally let the frustration out one Saturday night. "We have been down in this stinking basement for seventeen straight hours and we have nothing that resembles a solution to any of this. We have no suspects, no clues, no way to tie the crimes together. We have bupkis," he finally ejaculated in frustration.

"We have two clues," Paul corrected.

"What?" bellowed Dave.

"A bone fragment and a piece of a flint knife."

That was the end of his patience. Dave whirled around, standing in front of Paul gesticulating wildly. "You want to tell me one lousy piece of deer bone and a shard of flint from who knows what, are clues?" He threw the marker at the closest wall board and fell back into the torn upholstered chair at his back. He sat there a moment breathing hard in anguish for not having anything more now than seventeen hours earlier when this all started. He was clearly exhausted, pissed, and in need of something; but he had no idea what.

Paul was prepared for this. Without saying a word, he slowly rose from his own chair and walked deliberately to the small fridge in the corner of the basement. He opened the door and drew out two brown paper bags. Closing the fridge door with his foot, he turned and went over to Dave, who still sat huffing and puffing clearly unable to settle down. He reached down and placed one bag at his partner's side. Carrying the second bag, Paul walked over to the other chair and dropped into the sagging springs of his torn and tattered chair.

They sat lost in their own thoughts when Dave finally broke the silence and said, "What the hell is in the bag?"

Paul replied in one word, "Lubricant."

"Gheese." Dave uttered as he bent forward and retrieved the bag at his feet. It was heavy, and he could hear the sounds of glass clinking together as he resettled back in his chair. He continued to sit silently with the bag resting on his lap.

A minute later, he reached in and withdrew one of the bottles. Holding the cold dark colored glass bottle in his hand, he turned the bottle such that he exposed the face of a red dragon, the trademark insignia of The Demented Brewing Company of Middlesex New Jersey.

"Now that's what I call lubricant." He twisted off the cap and hoisted the brew toward his partner who performed the same ritual. Each then took a deep draw from their respective bottles and settled back in their chairs and stared once again at the array of macabre photographs arrayed across the white boards. Dave visibly relaxed, expressing his mood elevation with a deep sigh.

Paul knew what his partner needed, now he only hoped the lubricant would loosen up the gears and allow them to "think outside the box." He broke the silence and suggested they go over the crime scenes one more time.

Dave started. "Each crime scene had four victims."

"The first had five," Paul corrected.

"Five?"

"Yeah there were two adults, two children and a dog,"

"You and that damned dog. Okay, each scene had four human victims, while the first scene also included a dog. Satisfied?" queried Dave.

"Just want to make sure we don't overlook anything, sorry."

"Okay. "

Dave took a step toward the white boards, and walking from one to the other, he mused, "It appears from all counts that the male victim in each case was last to die and it is presumed that the male victim was directly responsible for the deaths of the remainder of the family."

'Yes, blood spatter from the first scene was found on the adult male, but no blood from the male was found on any of the other victims. The second scene was strangely devoid of blood. The blood spatter in the third scene was consistent with the first. The male was covered in the other's blood, but his blood was not on the other vics."

"Okay then, let's assume we have our killer in each case, the husband. But why?"

"Now that's the sixty- four-million-dollar question," bemused Paul, opening a second beer and tossing one to Dave. Looks like the lubrication was working; with Dave on a roll he wanted to keep it going.

"So, papa kills momma and the kiddies. Who kills papa?" asks Dave, writing on each board that the male kills each victim, then himself.

"Nope, big guy, papa does not kill himself,"

"Why not? Makes sense. Murder suicide, happens all the time," calls Dave somewhat satisfied with the solution.

"Okay, Sherlock, you may have a theory for cases one and two, but case three don't fit, "offered Paul. "In this case, the presumed murderer father had his heart cut out and we still can't find it. So, the theory doesn't hold true for all three cases. Maybe he does kill the wife and kiddies, but *who kills him?*"

"Well, there's that." Dave shrugged tossing the marker at Paul, who handily caught it.

"Yup, there's that."

"Okay then, what do you have, smart ass?"

"I agree, dad kills everyone. Why, I have no idea, but he kills everyone. Someone then has to kill him, right?

Victim number one splits his head open on the corner of the fireplace, maybe he trips or gets pushed by the wife, in any event he dies. Seems simple right?"

"You're on a roll, keep going," Dave calls out.

Paul steps up to the board for scene two. Tapping with the marker for emphasis says, "Here we see the father kills everyone and appears to set himself on fire, self-immolation, neatly covering up any clues he may have left behind. Murder/ Suicide at first glance makes sense, but then the good Dr. Howell throws in a ringer; papa two dies from a head injury, before he sets himself on fire. She also recovers a bone fragment, from what appears to be a two-hundred-year-old deer." Paul taps his marker on the bag containing the bone fragment. "So now we know that male number two could not have killed himself, pointing to the obvious conclusion that someone else was present" Paul continued tapping his marker on the whiteboard as he spoke each word for emphasis. "This is not a murder/ suicide, it is just plain murder."

On a roll, Paul heads to the third white board and continues. "In this final case, we have the most probable scenario in which the husband kills the family, but the evidence points conclusively to the fact he could not have killed himself for his heart was removed. No easy feat for a suicide to accomplish. So, there is only one likely conclusion, someone killed these three families and tried to make it look like the father did the deed. We have a murderer, who leaves no trace behind."

"So then, Watson, do you want me to believe we are looking for a ghost?" Dave snorted.

"Well, maybe," whispered Paul as he returned to his seat and opened the sixth and final beer in his bag. Guess the lubricant was working. Paul was indeed thinking outside the box. He was also thinking outside this very plane of existence.

Dave drained his final beer as he slumped in his chair. He sighed and then barely above a whisper he commented, "A ghost, what next."

Chapter 22

A full moon rose brightly over the Cook College Campus, lighting Passion Puddle with a shimmering mirror image of the orange moon. The stately trees whispered as they swayed in the light warm summer breeze. A few birds were chirping in the bushes. It was a beautiful and peaceful night.

I left the house on Seaman Street at a little after 11p.m. I had plenty of time before the appointed hour, so I decided to take a walk around campus to prepare my head and heart for whatever was to come next. So, I headed over to the Commons, passed through Greenhouse row, where I caught the petunia fragrance called Evening Scentsation, properly named for its fragrant. It blooms open only in the evening where the scent can be carried on the evening breeze. I filled my nostrils with the lovely scent while passing over to Lipman drive. I stood across from my lab at Thompson Hall, staring at the basement door as if it were a lover, one that I would never see again. I had no idea why I had suddenly become morose. I literally shook it off, turned and headed out of campus and toward Tabor House.

My journey was lit by the full moon, now having risen high in the sky. It shone so brightly it was as if it had become an evening sun whose cold heart light robbed us of color. I soon reached the front door to Tabor House and stood for a moment observing the Christogram announcing this was a house of God. I took a deep breath, let it out slowly and, with much trepidation, reached out and touched the doorknob, hoping against hope it was locked.

Of course, it was not. The door swung open noiselessly on well-oiled hinges and there I was once again in the entrance way. The room was dark save what light came in from the front windows. I looked to my left and was greeted by the lights that were on in the library. Once again, I took a deep breath, let it out slowly and headed toward the light.

I entered the library and saw it was empty. There was a single light lit on the end table casting a warm glow about the room. Having come from the cold light of the moon, it felt welcoming. I stood at the entrance taking in the room, casting my eyes over the myriad of books stacked neatly within the three walled bookshelves. I have always been amazed at the mass of literature these shelves contained. There were books of every size and color, all with spines swept of dust and perfectly aligned one next to the other. I soon became lost in my thoughts as I gazed about the room.

Out of the silence, I heard a familiar voice say "Welcome, I am pleased you have returned."

I turned toward the sound and there sat Ezerial, folded neatly in his favorite chair. I did not say a greeting in return but stood silent for a split second taking in is visage.

He was indeed remarkably handsome. He was tall, standing well over six feet two, perfectly proportioned from head to toe. His luxurious nearly jet-black hair was perfectly combed save for a wave that fell perfectly across his broad forehead. His eyes were a bright blue and seemed to look not at you but directly into your soul. His clothes this evening were more casual than usual. Instead of a well-tailored suit, this evening he wore a pure white turtleneck linen shirt, over black slacks.

105

He completed his wardrobe with red socks and highly polished black leather shoes. He was a vision of perfection. If there was ever someone who could model as an angel, it would be him. Then I remembered, he need not model an angel.

It seemed like an eternity to me before I responded to his greeting, but he did not indicate a concern. I politely replied, "Good evening, I am at your service."

Ezerial smiled a most beguiling smile, brushed his right hand through the unruly curl and elegantly, without the hint of effort, rose from the chair, and said "Good, then let us begin."

Chapter 23

"Have you been following the recent spate of murders that have befallen our community?"

"Of course," I replied, "the newspapers are filled with reports, suppositions and theories while besmirching the police for their inability to solve these hideous crimes."

"They will never solve these crimes," he reported matter-of-factly.

"What? How do you know?"

"Do you forget my vocation? "

My response was silence. Ezerial walked toward the bookshelf. "I have, shall we say certain, ah, certain abilities. I have access to knowledge, observations, information not readily available to anyone. My sources stretch far and wide, and, as you well know, extend beyond this mortal plane."

Of course, he was a Watcher, one of the few Enochian Angels sent by the Almighty to observe, watch and protect man. They were not to interfere, but as I well knew, Ezerial was not always obedient to the prime directive.

Ezerial continued, "The perpetrator of these hideous crimes is not one that the authorities have experience with. They are well prepared to investigate, collect evidence, draw conclusions and reconstruct the crime; all leading to capture the person or persons responsible for the criminal actions. However, in this case the *criminal* is not a person."

"What?" I ejaculated. "How can that be? What do you mean, *not a person?*"

"Robbie, you of all people should understand. You who have once lived and died and now live again. You were once dead for over 100 years, yet here you sit, with a newly minted corporeal body. You of all people should understand and accept that not all is visible, yet all can be altered given the proper circumstances." Silenced by his chastisement, I knew what he said was true. I did once live; a long, long time ago. I died on my twenty- fifth birthday, but I refused to be dead. Thus, I remained for over 100 years as a form of energy. Some would call my condition 'ghostly,' but I was no ghost. In life, I was strong, and in death, I was stronger. I was able to hold on to my life energy, drawing from my environment, avoiding the living and the dead as much as possible, I was able to remain on this plane as a being in a different state; not alive but certainly not dead.

It was when I was about to "give up the ghost," I met Ezerial the first time. He offered me the opportunity to possibly regain my corporeal body, if I would help him contain another angel, this time the renegade Azazel, who was hell bent on destroying our world. Through a nearly impossible quest, Ezerial sent me to another time and place where I was able to contain Azazel and return to this time and place with my current form. And so YES, I do understand and accept that there are things in this world that are well beyond what we can see and feel.

As if he could read my mind, Ezerial offered, "Good. I see you understand; shall we proceed?"

"Of course." I sat down on the Edwardian Wingback chair and prepared to open my mind to what Ezerial had to say.

"Good. Let us begin. Do you know the history of area where the crimes have been perpetrated?"

I shook my head.

"Let us start there."

Ezerial walked over to the bookcase and withdrew from the volumes a selection that appeared to be quite old. The book was bound in cloth, stretched tight and dyed a deep dark green. He opened the book and read aloud,

"Middlesex County, New Jersey is located midway between Boston and Washington D.C. (also midway between New York City and Philadelphia). It is in the center of the State of New Jersey, stretching from the Rahway River south to the Mercer and Monmouth County lines, and from the Raritan Bay west to the Somerset County line. The predominant geographic feature of the County is the Raritan River, which flows the entire width of the County from west to east (forming part of the Middlesex/Somerset County line) and is navigable from its mouth at the Raritan Bay to New Brunswick. The central location of the County and the presence of the Raritan River, within its boundaries, have been key factors in the original settlement and subsequent growth of Middlesex County.

The first known human inhabitants of Middlesex County were Native Americans known as the Lenni Lenape. Some oral traditions of the Lenape suggest that they themselves believed they were the original human inhabitants of the area. There is reliable

archaeological evidence to indicate that the Lenape, after migrating from the far west of North America, settled in Middlesex County at least 3,000 years ago.

The Lenape were part of the Algonquin language group. The tribal name, Lenape, can be translated, from the Algonquin language, to mean "Original People or True People" The nations of the Algonquin language group, as a whole, referred to the Lenape as "grandfathers," a term of respect indicating a belief that the Lenape were the original tribe of all Algonquin speaking peoples. The Lenape themselves believed that the Creator caused a giant turtle to rise from the depths of the ocean. The turtle grew until it became North America. The first Lenape man and the first Lenape woman sprouted from a tree which grew on the turtle's back. This creation myth is consistent with the Lenape belief that they were "the original people" inhabiting their lands.

Because of their status as the acknowledged "original people," the Lenape were often called upon to serve as intermediaries in disputes between rival tribes and to help resolve difficulties within the Algonquin Nation. Later, the Lenape also served as peacemakers between European settlers and Native Americans. The Iroquois tribes derisively referred to the Lenape as "the old women" because of their peaceful ways. The Lenape were farmers, fishermen and hunters."

He closed the book and turned to face me. I sighed and asked, "Interesting, but what does the history lesson have to do with the murders?"

"Everything."

After a moment of silence, I assume designed for me to take in all the information he just gave me, he continued. "As we can see, the Lenni Lenape were a peaceful people. Well respected by the other *human beings* that inhabited the area. That all changed with the arrival of the European invaders.

Reaching for another book, this was more like a pamphlet than a book, he turned to a page yellowed with age and read,

"The first European explorer to see New Jersey was probably the Italian navigator Giovanni Caboto, better known to most Americans as John Cabot. He sailed to North America aboard the 50-ton Matthew in 1497 for King Henry VII of England. It was upon Caboto's early explorations that later English claims to North America were based.

The first European explorer to enter the Raritan Bay and report on his contact with the native Lenape was another Italian, Giovanni da Verrazano. In 1524, Verrazano sailed to North America, aboard the Dauphine, for King Francois I of France.

From this point in time, life for the native American Indian changed forever, and not for the better. First the Dutch came and 'bought' land from the Lenape. These were not peaceful times for the invaders and the local Indians. The Dutch treated the Indian as an inferior, less than human. In the 1600's the aggressive and deceitful Hudson Bay Company came into the area, from Canada, fully prepared to rape and pillage the new world for its riches and natural resources.

The Indians were in the way of the HBC's expansionary plans. Using deceit, tricks and downright immoral dealings with the Indians, the HBC expanded their holdings far and wide. Many treaties and agreements were reached giving the HBC ownership of

more and more land and thus allow them to lay claim to more and more natural resources, reducing the ability of the Lenape to peacefully coexist with the 'white man'. In 1778 the HBC convened a conference to "enjoin with the local Indian population to develop a treaty to afford ownership of Native land to the HBC and so provide for our mutual benefit." We are not really sure how much of these treaties and land sales the Indians really understood. Non-Indians who were present at the negotiations have suggested that the work of the interpreters was somewhat deficient and perhaps deliberately deceptive. George Morgan, who was considered to be the Pennsylvanian most experienced in Indian affairs, did not participate in the conference and later wrote:

"There never was a Conference with the Indians so improperly or villainously conducted."

He closed the pamphlet and returned it to its position among the others on the shelf. Turning toward me, he said, "This was the beginning of the end for the Lenni Lenape people. From this time forward the invaders would mistreat them in ways far more brutal than reported in the history books. Now speaking from memory, perhaps a personal memory, Ezerial continued, "It was during the American Revolutionary War the fate of the Lenni Lenape was sealed. Set upon by Christian evangelists determined to Christianize these *heathens*, they descended in droves to spread the word." He stopped for a moment, lost in thought. Perhaps he was ashamed of the actions of these evangelists who were acting on "behalf of the Almighty."

Offering a whispered sigh, he continued, "Both the British and the Americans needed Native warriors to support their war effort. Despite the fact that the Indians readily supplied support, both the British and American armies mercilessly attacked and destroyed village after village. They killed every man woman and child in the most brutal ways possible. Hands and feet were cut off the women, after suffering the horrors of rape. Babies were dashed against stones or tossed off cliffs, not worth the cost of a bullet. The men were tortured, skinned or burned alive; their agony still rings in my ears. I was helpless to stop it. Forbidden.

He stopped talking and stood quietly before saying, "I apologize for my comment."

"That's all right," I offered, hoping to provide some level of sympathy. I had no real idea of what horrors Ezerial had witnessed at the hands of man against his own kind. Man is the cruelest of beasts, killing for sport or to gain advantage, savage and brutal beyond anything seen in the animal kingdom. It was a few moments before Ezerial was able to gather his thoughts and composure allowing him to continue.

"The attacks from both sides continued until summer 1782, when the Americans attacked once again. It was during this last battle at Killbuck Plains that the last surviving Wampum Belts and Bark Books, which contained all the written history of the Lenni Lenape were destroyed forever. The last of the Lenni Lenape, demoralized, decimated and suffering from disease such as smallpox, typhoid and other European contaminations, gave in and signed a peace treaty giving all their land to the Americans and their newly formed nation. Their fate was sealed."

Silence filled the room. I was confused as to what this history lesson had to do with the matter at hand. Clearing my throat, I asked, "I'm not sure how this has anything to do with the murders I thought we were here to discuss."

"It has everything to do with the murders. Shingas has returned and he seeks vengeance."

Chapter 24

A blood moon, the result of a lunar eclipse, where the moon passes through the earth's shadow, rose high over the Raritan River Conservancy. The warmth of the evening sun gave way to the cold dead light reflected off the orb of night. The moon glow lit the flowing river in an eerie reddish whiteness. The shallow waves played with the light casting images, lasting an instant, only to be lost as if a ghost were crossing the watery highway. The sounds of the water lapping against the shore were all that could be heard, for the silence was as deep as the river was shallow.

It was nearly the Twining Hour. As the ever-moving river of time ticked away the seconds, lost and never to return, we are condemned to move with the flow, ever forward.

The Twining Hour, some called it the Witching Hour, was the time when the energy of the living was at its lowest. It occurs each night around the hour of three a.m. when the living has retired to their beds. It is the hour when most machinery that powers the human civilization lays dormant, shut down, and silenced, if even for only a few hours, when it will be time to wake these mighty beasts from their slumber.

Even the animals of the field, having hunted for their food completed their meals. They have answered Mother Nature's imperative to mate, thus preparing for the next generation to come, and now they stop to seek shelter, lying in burrows or dens or high up in the trees. Their energy is reduced until a stillness falls over the land.

On this night, The Twining was powerful. The blood moon, full score and at the zenith of its travels, was shedding a light that was a reflection of life, rather than life itself. The time was near.

Once in every cycle or two, the Twining is so powerful that there is a slight rip in the fabric of time and space. The gossamer veil that separates this time and space from the time and space before and after is opened, if only for a moment. Then the fabric is repaired, and we are again safe from the things that are beyond.

On this night, the power of one that was long dead made his transition from the time of the dead to the time of the living. It was only a moment in our time, but near an eternity for one who has been dead for centuries.

The spirit, powerful for sure, but not yet powerful enough to sustain his energy to remain, stood once again at the shore of the mighty river, which he had once called home and walked among his people. The Medicine Man was but a whisper in the wind, not yet flesh and not yet fully formed, he was just a shimmer as the dead light bathed him in the light of the dead.

The land was silent. Even the river seemed too quiet, waves no longer tapping to the flow of time. If you were there, and especially attentive, perhaps you could hear the faint sound of prayer.

O Great Spirit of our Ancestors, I raise my face to you. I beg you look into my heart. I implore you to see the pain and the misery caused me in my time and place. I have witnessed the death and destruction of my people, the ones Ancestors called Original People.

116

The True People of the land where I now stand, were destroyed by the invaders from across the great oceans. They suffered horrors such that their spirit cannot rest. I beg you Ancestors look into my heart.

To you messengers, The Four Winds, and to Mother Earth who provides for her children, I beg you to give me the strength to do what must be done. Give me the power to return to the land of my people, to wreak vengeance upon those whose own ancestors destroyed my people. Grandfather, Great Spirit, once more behold me on this earth and lean low to hear my feeble voice. You lived first before the Ancestors. You are older than all need, older than all prayer. All things belong to you. Hear me, oh Grandfather, and give me the strength to do what must be done, to bring vengeance against those who destroyed your people and to allow me to turn them to dust, so your lands can be replenished with their blood.

I pray thee, Grandfather, lean in to hear my feeble voice. With tears running I beg thee Grandfather, give me the strength to nourish the tree that never bloomed. As I stand before its withered branches, let me nourish it with the blood of those who tried to destroy the tree at the root. I pray, that maybe some little root of the sacred tree is still alive, and that, with your help, we may see it bloom strong and proud as we, the Lenni Lenape, were once strong and proud.

And finally, O Great Spirit whose voice I hear in the winds and the river, whose breath gave life to all the world, give me life. I come before you small and weak. I need your strength and wisdom to do what must be done. Look down upon my brow and see your servant Shingas. Let me walk again amongst the living and behold the blood red sunset and the purple sunrise. I, Shingas, seek your strength, not for my own glory but for the glory of all your people. I beg thee,

Grandfather, grant me the power to become the Ghost Witch and let vengeance be mine.

Shingas repeated the prayer, delivered from the depths of his black heart, over and over again, beseeching the Great Spirit to hear him. At the end of each prayer, his spirit bowed before the rushing waters of the Raritan. He then fell on bended knee and cried out to be heard.

And so, it was, that the Great Spirit heard the plaintive pleas from Shingas. Lightning broke across the skies. Five immense bolts flew from east to west, once for each time Shingas delivered his prayer. That is how he knew the Great Spirit was pleased with him, and he was honored. When he finished his prayer for the last time his spirit remained on bended knee, facing the water.

As he remained prostrate in supplication before the Great Spirit, The Four Winds answered his call. The air grew fragrant from the scent of flowers unseen, as Shingas remained bowed, his body flat upon the ground before the red moon. The winds blew strong in answer to his pleadings. First the East Wind rustled the leaves in the trees whispering to Shingas, *I hear you*. The West Wind blew next, bringing the dry warm air across the Conservancy plain, telling Shingas, I see you. The mighty winds from the North blew next, cold and wet, saying to Shingas, *I love you*. Finally came the mighty winds from the South, filled with the scent of the prairies, long lost in this time and place, promising Shingas aid in his quest. Yes, indeed Mother Nature heard his call and responded with thunder, rolling over and over again across the plain. The Red Moon shone high in the skies, as the night

118

became day. Having heard the reply from the ancestral spirits, Shingas was much pleased.

To honor the Spirits further, Shingas danced the Circle Dance. To the Lenni Lenape, the circle dance was done to commemorate the gift of life, for life is a circle; we are born, we live, we die, and we are born again. The dance is also their gift to the Great Spirit who, with Mother Nature, is honored by the dance. Shingas wanted to be born again, but not of the flesh, but of the spirit, for as a spirit he could continue his plan to wreak vengeance on the living without fear of reprisal. He would be the perfect killing machine.

He danced first in silence. Then as the dawn was beginning to break, the animals of the field, waking from their slumber, heard his chanting and began to sing their songs, keeping time to the dance. The winds joined the chorus, as the leaves and tall grass of the plain rustled and swayed in time to the dance. Shingas was well please, but he knew his time was short. The sun had begun to show in the east. Dawn was upon him and sunrise was not far behind. He must return, once again, across the veil, back to the land of the dead. He must continue to gather his strength. He knew others must die, to increase his spirit energy, so that when the time came, he would be ready. Ready to cross the veil and become the Ghost Witch.

Chapter 25

A slight haze clung to the tall grass along the banks of the Old Raritan where Jeanne and Dave walked their beloved boxer pup, Misty, along the trails in the Conservancy. The couple, having retired a few years ago, enjoyed a daily brisk morning walk, after breakfast, along their favorite trails that clung to the riverbank. The Raritan waters flowing along the riverbank added a soothing sound. Most days they were alone to enjoy the peace and quiet in the early morning. Misty would often run ahead, find something, and bring it back to Dave, who would then give her a loving cuff under her chin and send her off on her next hunt. Jeanne would sometimes take photos of the landscape or newly blooming wildflowers, from which she would make a collage to hang in the bathroom.

As they continued to walk through the fields, everything was serene, peaceful. That all suddenly changed.

Misty was running along the riverbank and suddenly stopped, sniffed the air, and jumped into the tall grass. She started barking at something on the ground up ahead. It wasn't her usual playful bark, but a bark that was more excited, almost demanding.

"What's got Misty in a huff?" Jeanne asked Dave. "She's not usually so spooked."

"Ah, she probably found a dead rabbit or something. You know she is too chicken to touch anything dead. She is just calling us over to pick it up for her," replied Dave.

"Come on, Misty, quit your barking. You'll wake the dead and it's too quiet for all that noise," shouted Dave. "Get back here. C'mon girl, it's time to get home anyway."

Misty ignored her master and kept up the ruckus. If anything, she was more excited and was now jumping in a circle and barking excitedly at the same time. It looked as if there was something on the ground, something big, that had her attention, but she was too wary to get too close.

"Looks like I am gonna have to pull her off whatever it is," complained Dave, as he left the trail and entered the high grass. "Misty, get over here now!" he commanded.

Jeanne was close behind, interested in discovering what had Misty all excited. Stepping deeper into the tall grass, she froze behind Dave who had abruptly stopped. Jeanne pushed past her husband to get a better view and immediately regretted it. "My God!" was all she could call out before turning to Dave's side and emptying her breakfast all over the ground. Dave, who had worked in a hospital and was used to seeing gore on a daily basis, saw his wife vomit and he joined in. Misty just sat quietly next to the body.

Within the hour, Detectives Paul Mercuri and Dave Delair were on the scene. The entire area was closed off with yellow police tape, making a haphazard effort to keep the crime scene clear. Both Paul and Dave harbored secret thoughts that, just like the other scenes, there would be no clues here.

The coroner's office had sent Dr. Howell to the scene. She was garbed in rubber booties, rubber gloves, and hard hat. She wore a tight-fitting jumpsuit with Coroner neatly written in white letters across her back. Dave couldn't help but enjoy the view a minute too long. Paul noticed Dave's staring and threw an elbow into his partner's side to break his trance.

"Well, Doc, whatta we have here? "Dave said as he peered over the doctor's shoulder.

This time it was Dave who almost tossed his cookies. There before him laid the naked figure of what appeared to be man, or an animal of some kind. Catching his gore in his throat, Dave looked a little closer and confirmed, sure enough, it was a human. But something was wrong, horribly wrong. The body's arms were at shoulder height stretched tight and staked to what looked like wooden pegs. His legs were separated as far as they could go, also stretched tight and similarly staked to the ground. The problem was the body appeared to be covered from head to toe, front and back, with a fine mist of blood.

Dr. Howell, still on her knees examining the body, uttered, "Amazing." She was taking photographs from every angle, top and bottom views. As she took each photo, she stood a moment, reviewed the digital image on the camera, then shook her head, and simply said "Amazing" over and over.

Paul, who knew enough to stay back a little so as not to get the full effect of the scene, kept his head in the game and asked, "Oh, Doc. Thoughts?"

"Well, if I had to guess at this point, we have a deceased male about mid-sixties, nude, staked to the ground and missing his skin."

122

"What!" exclaimed both detectives. "How can he be missing his skin?"

"That will have to wait for the lab report, but from what I can see, his skin was removed in what appears to be a single sheet. I see no marks, such as peeling or cutting of the skin from the muscle. In fact, I see no cutting of the muscle anywhere. It looks as if the skin was carefully peeled right off the muscle, leaving the stratum germinativum or basal layer of skin on the muscle."

"I have no idea what that means, but it sounds sick." Dave wiped his brow with the back of his hand.

"Sick maybe, but until right now, I would have said impossible," whispered Dr. Howell, mostly to herself.

It was at least another hour before the geek squad turned over the scene, finding absolutely nothing. The coroner called in the gurney and the body was removed, leaving a sickly ooze on the ground. The stakes were pulled up and, just before they were put away, Dr. Howell called to the technician, "Let me see that rope on that stake, please."

The tech walked over and handed the stake over to her gloved hand. "Fascinating," she whispered, as she turned the stake over and over again in her hands. She looked closely at the spit of rope that was still attached to the stake.

She pulled a magnification glass out of her pocket and closely examined the rope with a deep fascination. She held it up to the light to get a better look and said, "If I didn't know better, I would say this rope was made of Indian hemp or dogbane."

She carefully placed a short length of the cordage between her fingers and rolled it back and forth until the fibers separated.

"Look here," she said, as she motioned to the technician. Dave and Paul also stepped closer to see what she found. "There seems to be something mixed in with the natural fibers. Indians in this area used to make cordage out of plant fibers mixed with evergreen roots with added animal sinew or rawhide for strength. "

"What are you saying? "Paul looked closely at what the doctor had in her hand.

"I'm saying that this cord looks like it was made by an Indian."

Chapter 26

For the next ten days, Delair and Mercuri spent every waking minute investigating the grisly murders. They knew, but had no proof, that the murders must be connected; they were perpetrated by the same person or persons, and they had no clues that could lead them to a suspect.

Most of the time was spent in Paul's mother's basement, affectionately known as the 'War Room.' "How in the hell can someone do so much damage, wreak so much havoc, leave behind so many bodies, and not one trace of evidence? No footprints, no hair samples, no fingerprints, no nothing," lamented Dave as he downed another Demented Brew.

"We do have a trace, remember?"

"No, enlighten me," Dave called to Paul as he opened the fridge to get another brew.

"In the first case we have nothing, true, but after that we have the following: a shard of animal bone, a sharpened piece of flint, and now we have cordage and stakes from the latest crime," Paul said, ticking off each item on his fingers.

"So?"

"So, if I had to look at the evidence and nothing else..."

"Okay, Sherlock, who did it?" chided Dave.

"I have no fuckin' idea," sighed Paul as he dropped into the chair and again faced the whiteboard. Sitting there a moment, he repeated, "I have no idea."

Just then the phone rang.

Paul reached for it. When David heard it was Dr. Howell, he wished he had gotten there first. For some reason, he could not get the lovely doctor out of his head. Any chance to speak with her, even if it was about these heinous crimes, was worth the cost.

"Detectives, come to the lab. I have some additional information you may find of interest. Perhaps it may even help you in the investigation." Before Paul could respond, Howell had hung up the phone.

Paul just stared at the handset for a moment, wondering how someone so pretty could be so clueless when it came to people skills. He dropped the phone back in the cradle. No cell phones in Mother Phyllis' house. "If a corded phone was good enough for me, it's good enough for you, "she would proclaim.

Still chuckling to himself, Paul said, "It looks like we have been summoned to the realm of the good Doctor Howell once again."

Dave, smiling a little to himself, pleased to get to see Howell again, responded, "Well then, let's not keep the good doctor waiting, shall we?" He bounded up the basement stairs, followed by Paul, who just shook his head knowing his partner was infatuated with Dr. Howell. Who was he to stand in the way of "love" anyway?

Dave jumped behind the wheel and, before Paul had the door fully closed, Dave had already started the car and was backing out of the driveway.

Paul turned to Dave. "What's the rush big guy?"

Dave just turned, smiled, and stepped on the gas a little harder.

Chapter 27

Once again, at the appointed hour, I arrived at Tabor House. The evening air was sultry, unusual for this time of year. The moon still shone full and had an eerie color. Something was wrong, I could feel it, but I had no idea what. It was just a feeling and it made me concerned, if not a little scared.

I came to the front door and it was unlocked as usual, the only light, of course, was in the library. Ezerial was there, uncharacteristically pacing in front of the great bookcases. There was something about his pacing. He was clearly agitated; his brow was furrowed. As I entered the room, he stopped pacing, and, turning toward me, said, "Robbie, I am afraid things are escalating at a most rapid pace. We must discuss a plan to stop Shingas before his power grows to the extent whereby he becomes impossible to stop."

I stood there for a moment and studied him. He looked different as he uttered these words. His hair was unkempt. His clothes were wrinkled. He no longer wore a suit but was dressed in a white turtleneck and black pants. I thought I even saw a spot of sweat on his brow.

"What's wrong? "I asked.

"Last night, as you well know, Shingas struck again, killing on the banks of the river. Shingas has been gathering the energy of those he kills, holding their life force, binding their energy to his, so that soon, when he gathers enough energy, he will be able to pass through the veil of death and come into this world and seek his vengeance." He spoke without pause.

"How can an Indian Shaman, who has been dead for nearly 200 years, come back?"

"First, Shingas was not a shaman, he was a medicine man," Ezerial replied resuming his usual lecturing tone.

"What's the difference?"

Ezerial walked calmly over to the bookcase and once again withdrew a book from a middle shelf. He opened it and began to read in a most scholarly tone.

"A shaman, unlike the Native American Indian medicine man, is someone who is regarded as having access to, and influence in, the world of benevolent and malevolent spirits. In order for the shaman to practice his vocation he must first enter a trance state during a ritual. He may take herbs, drink various teas made from roots or mushroom, or consume other spoils in order to reach the required trance state. While in this altered state, the shaman practices divination and healing. The word "shaman" probably originates from the Tungusic Evenki language of North Asia, and may have roots that extend back in time at least two millennia. The term was first introduced to the west after Russian forces conquered the shamanistic Khanate of Kazan in 1552.

The term "shamanism" was first applied by western anthropologists as outside observers of the ancient religion of the Turks and Mongols, as well as those of the neighboring Tungusic and Samoyedic-speaking peoples. Upon observing more religious traditions across the world, some western anthropologists began to also use the term in a very broad sense, to describe unrelated magico-religious practices found within the ethnic religions of other parts of Asia, Africa, Australasia and even completely unrelated parts of the Americas, as they believed these practices to be similar to one another.

"While Non-Native anthropologists sometimes use the term "shaman" for Indigenous Healers worldwide, including the Americas; "shaman" is the specific name for a spiritual mediator from the Tungusic peoples of Siberia and is not used in Native American or First Nations communities."

Closing the book, he glared at me as if I somehow, I offended him. I didn't know what to say so I apologized for my ignorance.

"I assure you, we are not dealing with a shaman or healer of any kind. What we have is worse, much worse," he continued to lecture as he returned the reference to its proper position on the shelf. Turning toward me once again, he passed his hand through his black hair and repeated, "Much worse."

"Well, then, what exactly are we dealing with here?" I asked, somewhat frustrated at this evening's discourse.

Sensing my heightened emotional state, Ezerial appeared to change before my very eyes. His entire countenance relaxed. His shoulders mellowed. He remained perfectly erect with his self-assured straight posture, but he looked softer, more like his old self.

Slowly and deliberately, as is his custom, he glided toward his chair and once again folded his frame into the soft leather. Then, folding his hands in that most peculiar way of his, breathed a deep sigh. He was now fully recovered and prepared to continue our discussion in his more natural, peaceful state.

After a moment of silence, I asked, "If it's not a shaman, we are dealing with, then what is it?"

He hesitated a second or two, removed his hands from under his chin, and spoke clearly. "I am afraid what we have here is a Skadegamutc or Ghost Witch."

"What the hell is that?"

"Of course, I wouldn't expect you understand the nature of the term. Let me explain." Ezerial remained seated in his chair. "We are dealing with a Skadegamutc, or Ghost Witch, an undead monster of the Native American Indian tribes. His name is Shingas and he was once a very powerful leader of the Lenni Lenape Indian tribe who lived in this very area. Usually, a Skadegamutc is said to have been created upon the death of an evil magician who refuses to stay dead but comes to life to seek his vengeance upon the people who wronged him in life. In order to destroy the risen Ghost Witch, it is said, you must return his energy to the universe from whence it came."

I was shocked into silence. A Ghost Witch? Some dead Indian medicine man, dead some two hundred years, has returned to seek vengeance.

Before I could utter another word, Ezerial simply said, "Yes, you are correct."

"So, then we are dealing with an evil spirit, right?"

"Yes, and more."

"So, to deal with an evil spirit all we need is an exorcism, and who is more eminently equipped to perform one than you, an Enochian Angel?" I said, all too happy to have solved the problem.

"Not quite."

"Whatta you mean?"

"If it were as simple as an exorcism, I would not have been required to solicit your help in dealing with Shingas. I have performed many successful exorcisms, and am well equipped to perform another, but there is one requirement lacking in this case."

"Lacking? What could possibly be lacking?" I said, incredulously.

"Belief in the Christian God"

"I don't understand."

"Let me try to help with that." Ezerial resumed his lecture persona and continued. "In order for an evil spirit, or for that matter any spirit or so-called demon, to be removed by an exorcism there must be some preconceived understanding that God has a power over the spirit."

I thought about that for a minute. "I see, go on."

"An exorcism is a religious or spiritual practice allowing the exorcist, who claims dominion over the evil spirit, the ability to evict said demons or other spiritual entities from a person or object or area they are believed to have possessed. Depending on the spiritual complexities of the exorcist, this may be done by causing the entity to swear an oath, performing an elaborate ritual, or simply by commanding it to depart in the name of a higher power. The practice is ancient and part of the belief system of many cultures and religions. Unfortunately, if the entity does not believe in, or otherwise respect the higher power, then the exorcism is doomed at the start. "

"So, you are saying that this Shingas will not leave because he does not fear a Christian God, and therefore an exorcism will fail?" My emotions were rising again.

"Precisely."

With both of us lost in thought, the room was silent. Ezerial sat as if he had turned to stone. He was staring directly into my eyes, as if he were telling me something, that, as yet, I could not hear. I could bear it no longer. "Okay, then what can we do?"

Smiling, Ezerial replied, "That, Dr. Mauro, is where you come in."

"Me?" I said incredulously. "What can I do that you can't?"

Ezerial smiled for the first time and uttered a single word. "Die."

Chapter 28

It was as if he punched me in the stomach. I couldn't contain my myself. I exploded out of my chair. I was excited, outraged, and angry all at the same time.

"Die!" I screamed. I began ranting and raving, waving my arms like a maniac, lashing out at Ezerial. I continued, "You want me to die! Are you crazy! Why in the hell would I ever do that?" I screamed. I turned and faced him, standing fully erect as he remained seated. My eyes bore deep into his as my hands clenched in fists of rage. My body was on fire, I was sweating profusely. I was breathing hard, short breaths like a bull in the arena, ready to pounce but not ready to die. My face was flushed, my heart pounded, my ears rang. I could hear my own blood pounding in my head. I stood there clenching and unclenching my fists in a rage that was nearly well beyond control. "Die! You want me to die?"

He never moved. He sat there silently as if we were discussing Shakespeare. His eyes followed my antics about the room, but he barely moved his head. His relaxed demeanor enraged me even more. When I saw his reaction, or more plainly, his lack thereof, I was set off again. "I can't believe what you just asked of me. "I moved closer to the seated Ezerial, but not too close. I was concerned of what his reaction might be if I got too close. I was confused, and more than a little afraid.

The adrenaline that was coursing through every fiber in my body had me on high alert. I was flushed a bright red, unable to control myself. I lashed out once more "Die! NEVER!"

Exhausted, I fell back in my chair. Breathing hard, slumped deep into the soft leather, I gripped the armrests as if I were on a bucking bronco. Through my shallow breaths I was able to mutter, "Outrageous. He wants me to die, AGAIN!" I remained in the chair, shuddering from overwrought nerves, muttering to myself. After a while, my breathing became less shallow. I loosened my grip on the leather armrests, leaving deep finger gouges I hoped would soon fade. My body slowly adjusted to normal. I was dripping with sweat and felt like I had done a few rounds with Mike Tyson. I looked over at Ezerial; he never moved. He was as a statue. I felt my blood beginning to boil once again.

"I am sorry," was all he said.

"And that makes me feel so much better," I returned with sarcasm. "I am not going to die. Period."

"Perhaps I have not made it clear the magnitude of the situation. Shingas was a very powerful and well-respected medicine man by the indigenous people. He was a healer and charismatic leader and, therefore, his death at the hands of American soldiers was, to say the least, a tragedy. Much like you, Shingas was not ready to die, and so he used his knowledge and powerful spirit to cross over from time to time to this plane of existence, waiting. He was angry, and he used this anger to create a spirit on the dark site of death. He became a Ghost Witch, as I have explained before, but I have not explained what that means."

Ezerial sat there a moment contemplating what to say next. I was silent waiting for him to continue.

"The Ghost Witch is a rare entity that forms when a powerful spirit is so damaged by anger that it becomes pure evil incarnate. Most would define the entity as a demon, one that desires only revenge on those who wronged it. In this case, Shingas has grown more powerful with each murder. He is absorbing the life energy from each of his victims. Soon, he will be powerful enough to cross the veil that separates this world from the other. His goal is to cross over permanently, not in a corporeal form, but as a demon spirit able to interact with, yet not be seen by, the living. But that is not the true danger."

"The true danger lies in when he is crossing over. Shingas will leave open a door from his realm into ours, making it easier for other angry spirits to cross over, flooding our world with pure evil. That is why we need to stop Shingas before he crosses. And only you, with your unique spirit, may be strong enough to stop him. That is why I am enlisting your assistance, for without your help, all may be lost."

I stared at Ezerial, trying to figure out what to do. I was not going to die to stop some Ghost Witch. I couldn't see how my dying could possibly do any good anyway. I had no idea what to say or do next, so I said nothing and just sat there. It seemed like hours before either of us moved. Ezerial was the first to break the silence.

"Of course, I can see now that it was beyond my bounds of prudence to ask such of you, but in the end, I saw no other way. I can understand your reluctance to participate in this venture, but we must stop Shingas from coming over. We cannot allow that door to be opened. What happens next is entirely up to you." Once again, he resumed his contemplative position, legs neatly crossed, fingers folded in his peculiar way with index fingers pointed under his chin. He just sat there, staring through me.

"Reluctance?" I queried. "You want me to die and you wonder if I'm reluctant?" I took a deep breath, trying to slow my rising pulse. "You bet I'm reluctant."

"Then, we are at an impasse."

Again, silence shook the room. Ezerial was a patient person, not given to emotion; in fact, I have rarely seen him smile or rise to anger. He just sat there, as if he were planning to do so for all eternity, waiting upon my next move. Through sheer force of will, I rolled my shoulders a few times I tried to loosen the knot that had formed in my neck, took in a deep breath and let it out in a long single blow, shook my head as if to say no, and replied, "So what exactly do you want me to do?"

Leaning forward, ever so slightly, he said, "Thank you."

Ezerial stood up from the chair and began to pace about the room. "We are going to need assistance."

"Assistance? From who?" I was stunned at the thought of bringing someone else into the fold of this adventure.
"For one, we will need someone who will kill you."
"Now, wait a minute. What do you mean, someone to kill me? I thought you would do that with your powers or something."

"For obvious reasons, it is against my nature as a Watcher to interfere in humanity, let alone kill someone. No, for that we will need a medical professional, one that not only will kill you effectively, without damage to your corporeal body, but one who can monitor your condition throughout the ordeal and then bring you back."

"Who?" was all I could say.

Without responding to my question, Ezerial continued, "We will also need to enlist the aid of people familiar with securing a location, so we are not disturbed during our efforts. We will need professionals familiar enough with the case, yet open minded enough to allow us to execute our plan while keeping all we do secret. I know exactly whom we can enlist to help us with our quest, but I will have to set in motion events that will bring them to our door, rather than having to seek them out." I still couldn't believe what was being asked of me.

Turning once again toward me, he continued, "I am going to need three days to prepare events, a time and place to execute our plan, and to secure the cooperation of others. I will need to move quickly and alone. Can you return here three days hence, precisely at midnight, your affairs in order, and your mind committed to the task at hand? In the meantime, there is much to do and precious little time to do it." With this, he left the room.

I was dismissed. I rose from my chair, looked about the room and breathed a deep sigh. And so, once again, I was planning to die.

Chapter 29

The phone rang in the war room and Paul just looked at it. He and Dave had been up most of the night reviewing the events surrounding the latest murder. "No identification of the deceased, no murder weapon, no trace; in fact, nothing left behind. Who the hell is this guy? A ghost?" Paul lamented as the phone continued to ring.

"Are you gonna get that or not?" Dave called out sarcastically as he made no effort to answer the phone himself, even though he was closest to it.

"Sure, why not; what else could go wrong?"

Paul picked up the receiver and, before he could say a word, he heard a voice on the line say, "Detectives, you better get here right away. I've ID'd the latest victim and you aren't gonna like it."

"Good morning to you as well, Dr. Howell," Paul said a little too sarcastically. He was tired, pissed, and hung over from too much lubrication the night before as he and Dave struggled to figure out what was going on. It was not like him to be so mean, but he was not feeling himself.

Dave reached out and twisted the phone out of Paul's hand, glaring at Paul in admonishment. "I'm sorry for my partner, Dr. Howell, but it was a long and very unproductive night, and I am afraid these murders are taking their toll on all of us."

"Well, if you think it was bad before, then you're going to be really unhinged when you see what I have found now."
"What?"

"Just get down here now. I'm not sure how long I can keep this information under wraps." And, without another word of explanation, Dr. Emily Howell hung up the phone.

"Get up," Dave said. "We have once again been summoned by the good doctor. She has something big. I have no idea what, but she wants us there pronto. So, get up, try some mouthwash, and let's get going. The dead just can't seem to wait."

Paul rose from the chair as if he were much older than his twenty-nine years. He felt old. This case was driving him mad. He loved being a cop, and, he was good at it. However, there was something about this case. This case was not natural. Bodies found in horrific settings as if staged. No clues. No suspects. It was as if the killer, or killers, were demons. Impossible he knew, but that seemed the best explanation. Paul was not ready to give up, but, unless something were to break, and break soon, he knew that they were going to need help from some outside source to get a handle on what was happening. He was, however, not yet ready to share his feelings with his more experience and grounded partner Dave. That would have been a rookie mistake, and open Paul up to ridicule throughout the department. So, Paul kept quiet, washed his face, chugged on the Scope to cleanse his breath, and followed Dave up the stairs into the bright sunlight. By noon, their day would become much darker.

Chapter 30

The detectives arrived at the morgue and signed in as is procedure. They headed down the hall toward the locker rooms to change into lab gowns. Dr. Howell had always insisted on this practice to keep her surgical field sterile. Ordinarily cops didn't always follow this procedure, but Dave wanted to get, and stay, on Emily's good, side so he followed her requests, or at least made an attempt. As they were heading towards the locker room to change, they were stopped by a most agitated Dr. Howell.

"Follow me."

"Don't we need to cover?" asked Dave, a little surprised at the abruptness.

"Not where we're going. C'mon, this way." Dr. Howell turned down a side hall.

Dave and Paul trotted a few quick steps to catch up with Dr. Howell. Having gained her side, Dave asked, "Where are we going?"

"The basement. We have some of the original surgical suites down there from when we first opened the morgue. It's outdated, and not used anymore, just for tours when we want to scare the bejesus out of teens who are on a path that will send them there long before their time."

"I see."

"Most importantly, it's secluded, and I didn't want anyone to see what I discovered until we had a plan."

Before Dave could query Dr. Howell further, she turned a corner and hit the doors to the stairs and down they went into the bowels of the building.

It was obvious, this was an older part of the building as they descended the worn and filthy stairs towards the first landing. The bright LED's from the main floor gave way to older fluorescent lighting fixtures that hung in a line across the ceiling. Dr. Howell hit a light switch at the foot of the landing. The system responded with a flickering of lights accompanied by an incessant buzz from ancient ballast units awakened from sleep for who knew how long. When the flickering finally stopped, the yellowed glow from the ancient tubes steadied to reveal a long, somewhat foreboding, hall. The fixtures were designed to handle two forty-eight-inch fluorescent tubes each. Most held only one, and in many cases none. The normally white light afforded by the bulbs had turned a darker yellow from age and grime. This gave a very eerie pallor to the hall, giving the impression of a cheap Hollywood horror set. Except this was no movie set; it was real. It gave Dave the creeps.

"This is the original morgue unit, built back in the day when we wanted to keep the dead hidden from the public," Dr. Howell began as if conducting a tour. "This area has been closed for more than ten years. We moved to more modern facilities upstairs when the building was renovated. At that time, Dr. Alex Methuen was Chief, and he wanted to preserve these suites, so we could remember from whence we came. And now I am glad he did. This way," directed Dr. Howell as she pushed through a pair of dusty swinging doors whose glass was so dirty that one could not see through them.

They entered what appeared to be an ancient surgical suite. The walls were covered floor to ceiling with ancient green tiles, many missing, some cracked, and all covered with a fine film of filth. The room itself was dark and had that medicinal smell you find in hospitals and funeral parlors. Dave and Paul stopped at the swinging doors, not sure they wanted to proceed any further into the depths of this hell hole. Dr. Howell pressed straight into the room, beckoning the others to follow. Dave looked at Paul, who shook his head and looked down at the floor. Dave took a deep breath, immediately regretting it, and they both entered the chamber of horrors.

The walls were filthy, cobwebs in the corners and something odorous coming from who knows where or when. Dave choked back a gag. Dr. Howell ignored him, hit a light switch on the wall, and beckoned the two detectives forward.

They stopped a few feet from the center of the room where something lay covered with a grimy yellowed sheet on a surgical table. The detectives hesitated as the drew closer.

Howell removed the sheet revealing the skinless body from the last murder. The detectives jumped back a step when Dr. Howell spoke again. "Gentlemen, I give you the Colonel, New Brunswick's most famous citizen.

Chapter 31

John Neilson, affectionately known as "The Colonel" throughout New Brunswick, was a direct descendant of the original Colonel John Neilson, who on July 9th, 1776, gave one of the earliest readings of the Declaration of Independence to a crowd in the town square of New Brunswick, New Jersey.

Born March 11, 1745, in the busy port community of Raritan Landing across the Raritan River from what is now the Westons Mills area, Neilson was raised by his uncle James Neilson, one of the first settlers and businessmen in New Brunswick. Neilson's father died when he was an infant. His mother died a year later. If not for his uncle, John might have been sent to an orphanage, into a life of drudgery, and, most likely, an early death.

John grew up a staunch believer in the American dream. As a businessman, he spoke loudly against the oppression wrought on the colonies by the Crown. He owned a tavern, coffee house, and several millinery shops. He was quite prosperous and more than a little dogged when it came time to pay taxes to the Crown. His treasonous speeches against taxation, formed the basis for our Declaration of Independence.

New Brunswick continued to flourish and grew to become a well-known Colonial trading hub. The prosperous city became a crossroads for travel and trade, so John had an ever-growing audience for his tirades against colonial rule. His stature as an outspoken proponent against the British led most local historians to say the Neilson house, on Burnet Street, had become "a haven for revolutionary activity."

At the age of twenty-nine, John joined the New Jersey militia and was soon commissioned a Colonel where he led one of two regiments of the Middlesex County Militia. He fought bravely against both the British and their Indian allies. He worked closely with George Washington, gaining both favor and wealth in the process.

On a summer day in 1774 under the command of Colonel John Neilson, the Middlesex County Militia met, and defeated, a contingent of British and Indian allies, who had approached the city from a portage along the river to the east of downtown. It was said the fighting was fierce, but the British were soundly defeated and many surrendered. The soldiers were taken to a prisoner encampment in Trenton a few miles to the South. The Colonel, however, took a different tact with the Indians. He ordered them slaughtered. The militia obliged and bayoneted the Indian braves to save precious ammunition. It was reported in the Brunswick Gazette the next day that "the river ran red with native blood."

At the end of the war, Neilson was asked to join the First Continental Congress as it drafted the Declaration of Independence in Philadelphia. John was not a statesman, nor did he want to abide by the customs and intrigues of politics. Neilson, therefore, declined the honor, claiming his duties to New Brunswick were all he could handle. As a reward for his service, he was given a copy of the first printing of the Declaration, which he famously read while standing on a tavern table in the town square.

The modern John Neilson carried on the family name and was a successful businessman, former Mayor of New Brunswick, and instrumental in deeding the land around the Raritan River to become the Conservancy, where he met his brutal death. John was known to all as an upstanding citizen, whose brutal murder would not be taken lightly by the current city leaders.

Dave snapped out of his reverie and challenged Dr. Howell by asking, "Are you sure? How can you be sure?"

"I was able to confirm his identity through dental records. John had extensive dental work done by a local dentist. The confirmation came back this morning. Soon as I knew for sure, I called you two, and here we are."

"Who else knows this?" Paul asked speaking for the first time since the detectives arrived at the morgue.

"Far as I know, only the dentist, me, and now you two. I assure you, once this goes public, the hue and cry will be heard far and wide. The city elders will be calling for your heads on a platter."

"Jesus," was all Paul could mutter.

"How long can we keep this under wraps?" Dave began pacing around the room.

"A day, maybe two at the most."

"Okay, okay, we have forty-eight hours to find something or someone that can break this open. Dr. Howell, do you have any ideas, any ideas at all, no matter how crazy or outlandish, that could give us anything to work on?"

Emily stood for a moment contemplating her response. She looked over at the body, studying every feature, hoping to find something she might have missed. Finally, she looked at Dave and offered, 'From what I can tell, the skin was removed from the inside out. The connective tissue was melted, not cut away, literally, melted off the muscle and removed as if a sheet from a bed."

Dave gagged before asking, "What could do such a thing?"

Dr. Howell looked sympathetically at him. It was obvious she didn't want to cause him any more anguish; he looked beaten enough already. She bowed her head a little so as not to be looking directly into his eyes and said, "I am sorry. I truly am. But, in my experience as a doctor and a scientist, I have no idea what could have done this to a human body. There is no scientific explanation. There are no surgical scars, no chemical residue, no heat scorching, nothing natural that could result in a body being skinned from the inside out. I'm sorry, but I have no scientific explanation."

"Okay, then give me your gut feeling, not your science. If all things were on the table as an option, what would you guess?"

Dr. Howell coughed to clear her throat. "In my opinion, what we have here is unnatural. Therefore, we must look outside the real world, beyond, into the supernatural."

The detectives were stunned. Paul broke the silence. "I agree with Dr. Howell. Nothing makes sense. None of the murders seem natural. I don't like it any more than you do, but I think we need to look outside the box, way outside." Paul figured he was now open to ridicule from his partner after making such an outrageous suggestion.

Dave just stood there a moment, taking it all in. You could almost smell the smoke, as the wheels in his mind turned over and over again. He was rummaging through all the facts and suppositions, looking for a logical outcome for these heinous crimes. After a few moments, he said, "I agree. Anyone know a good exorcist? "

Chapter 32

The two days reprieve was not to be. Unfortunately for the detectives, the next morning *The Newark Star Ledger*, a sensationalistic rag printed in Newark and covering all the news about the area, printed the story. The headline was not kind and certainly added more pain to the beleaguered detectives' plight. Across the frontpage banner, plastered in large dark print read,

New Brunswick's Most Famous Citizen
Murdered by Unknown Assailants

Unfortunately, it was the next line that was the most damning:

Police Seek Help from Exorcist

Dave was fuming mad. "I thought we had some time before the story broke. Now we have nothing. The brass is gonna be all over us line stink on shit and we have nothing." He paced back and forth across the basement war room.

Paul knew his partner well enough not to say anything unless Dave released his wrath at him. So, Paul remained placid in the chair as his partner vented his rage. Underneath he was fuming mad as well.

The phone rang. Dave picked up to hear Dr. Howell whisper, "I'm sorry."

"You're sorry, Jesus. Who the hell spilled their guts? Jesus. What the hell do we do now?"

Dr. Howell continued, "When I saw the headlines, I was furious myself. I called a staff meeting and locked the doors, telling them that no one was leaving until I had an explanation of how the information got out. It took a few minutes of threats, but my diener finally confessed. He is young, stupid, and now unemployed."

"Damn!"

"Yes, damn. He was having a make-out session with one of the orderlies in the basement and overheard part of the discussion. He beat it out of there before we left, so we had no idea we were spied on."

"So, how did it get into the paper?" demanded Dave, still rattled and breathing in short breaths.

"He and his make-out buddy went to Tumulty's Pub last night and hoisted a few. One thing led to another and he told her everything. He must have been bragging a little too loudly because one of the newspaper reporters overheard him, and boom, here we are."

"Damn, damn, double damn," was all Dave could muster as he once again began pacing as far as the corded phone would let him.

"Did he have to open his mouth and say that 'the police are looking for an exorcist?' Jesus, the brass is gonna think we've lost our minds," shouted Dave, before calming down. "Dr. Howell, I am sorry. It was not your fault. Please, I am pissed and really shouldn't have taken it out on you."

"Please call me Emily. We are now in this together. It was my subordinate that put you in this position and I promise I will help get you out. "

Dave breathed a little easier, scratched his head, and turned around thinking. He ran his hand through his hair. "Okay, we still have nothing to work on. You, Paul, and I opened the door to a supernatural explanation. I may not like it, and the brass will hate it, but let's go through the door and see what is on the other side." He turned toward Paul and asked, "Are you okay with this?"

Paul was shocked. Dave was really going to be open to a supernatural explanation. What did that even mean? Who were they looking for? Did they need a priest or an exorcist? How is that gonna play out in the news?

"Paul, wake up. Are you in or not?" shouted Dave from across the room.

"I'm all in. We need to solve this puzzle before anyone else gets hurt."

"Okay then, next stop crazy town." Dave said goodbye to Emily and hung up. He looked at Paul. "What the hell are we going to do now?"

"I have no idea but, I'm sure this is going to get a lot worse before it gets any better," replied Paul.

"Amen," was Dave's only retort.

Chapter 33

I spent the next three days in my own private hell. I was going to die, again, and there seemed to be no way to avoid it. I was not in control of my own life. I didn't know what to do. Everything was spinning out of control and there was no end in sight, except one where I end up dead. I couldn't bear the thought of dying again.

In an effort to regain my composure and, hopefully, come to terms with what I was committed to do, I decided I needed to be alone, really alone.

I grabbed a few things and headed through the living room of my home on Seamen street and reached for the secret latch under the fireplace mantel. I pulled on the latch, which released a hidden lock and opened the clandestine door to my old loft. I hadn't been up there in years, but just climbing the stairs felt soothing. I just knew this was the right thing to do.

Slowly, I climbed the circular stone steps, counting them one at a time. My right hand felt along the cool smooth stones as I reached higher and higher into the loft. The sound of my shoes ringing off the flagstone steps was comforting. When I finally reached the top step I just stood there, partially on the staircase and partially in the room, not fully in either. It was as if I were not fully in this life or the next. I stood there and began to survey my surroundings.

Everything was exactly as I had left it decades ago. My old bed stood in the corner under an eve. The bedspread was as pristine as if I had just made the bed this morning. There was not a wrinkle to be seen. The two pillows were propped up against the headboard, beckoning me to come and lie down, rest. I was pulled toward the bed but held my ground on the stairs.

The floors, too, were spotless. I expected them to be covered with a fine layer of dust, but they were not. There were no crumbs or droppings from rodents I was sure inhabited the space. It was as if they were swept daily by some unseen hand. I was a little put off, frightened actually, but I entered the loft. I stood a few inches into the room and stopped once again. What was that sound? It was the quiet, almost imperceptible, yet unmistakable sound of a sigh. I quickly searched around the room, peering into the darkest corners, hoping to see something I knew was not there. Of course, no one was there. I replied with a sigh of my own and entered fully into the room.

Suddenly, everything changed. The harsh sunlight that poured in from the gabled widow's walk suddenly softened. The light reduced to a warm inviting glow, yet no clouds impeded the rays. It was as if the hand of God turned a rheostat and softened the light.

As I entered further, I could feel the very atmosphere in the room change, as if I were suddenly cushioned by a soft blanket there to insulate me from what was to come. I felt protected, my fear all but gone. I progressed further and there before me, in the exact center of the room was my grandmother's old bentwood rocker.

This was the same rocker that my grandmother rocked her children, including my father, to sleep in her arms. When my

153

father married my mother, one of their wedding gifts was this rocker. She told my father, "I rocked you to sleep in this chair, now you rock your children the same." And so, it was, that when I was but a babe in arms, my mother or father would sit in this chair, me in their arms and rock me to sleep. This chair held very fond memories of being held close, safe, in powerful arms protecting me from the world.

Nearly two hundred years old it stood there, pristine, as if it were lovingly made by hand yesterday. The rocker rested on an interwoven rug, the kind often used to protect a wood floor from the harsh workings of the wooden rocker. It stood facing the stairs, calling to me as if given voice. It actually sang to me, in my head, an old song my grandmother used to sing to me when I felt alone:

Come my baby Sit with me Come and sit upon my knee
I will hold you I will rock you I will love you on my knee

She would hold me on this very chair and rock me while singing in the most beautiful voice I had ever heard. Whatever ailed me or made me sad would soon be gone, for my grandmother would sing the pain away.

I stood a moment before her chair, fondly reminiscing about sitting with her and how good it made me feel. Without conscious movement on my part, my body moved gently toward the chair. I removed the pillow that was propped up on the back of the seat and sat down "on my grandmother's knee."

I sat and rocked, clutching the pillow, a gift from my grandmother, while humming the song in my head over and over. I was completely at peace. I don't know how long I sat there; I frankly didn't care. I was home, safe, held tightly by the spirit of my grandmother. I fell asleep.

The dream came quickly, more a vision than a dream. I could see before me my mother and father. My grandmother was also there. We were sitting around the old dining room table back in Brooklyn, except this time I was all grown up. I left my home in Brooklyn when I graduated high school, around eighteen years old, but in this dream, I was fully an adult.

I had the feeling it was a Sunday, in my vision. I recalled that we often sat around the dining room table talking, telling stories, laughing, enjoying life, and each other's company. It was always a happy time around that table, but in this moment, the atmosphere around the table was more somber.

I was afraid to speak or even move for fear I would chase the dream away, so I sat there, an observer in my own dream. My father was the first to speak.

"Robbie, we are so proud of you. You have done so much, yet there is something more you must do. I know it is hard. I know you are afraid, but we are here with you. You are not alone, my son. We are always here."

Before I could speak, my mother continued, "My dearest son, I love you with all my heart and soul. You were there for your father when I could not be. What you face now, you face not alone. We are with you now and always. Trust in those around you. They need your help. Only you can do what must be done. Have no fear for we are with you now and forever."

My grandmother was silent, but I could see love in her eyes. She smiled at me and nodded; no words were needed. I knew what must be done. Before I could say thank you, the dream faded. I startled awake almost falling from my chair. I was not alone in my quest. I made up my mind then and there to follow Ezerial to the ends of the earth to stop Shingas from opening the door to the other side. If it cost me my life, my very soul, no matter. I was not alone; my family was waiting for me. With that support, I knew I would not fail.

I rose from the rocker, replaced the pillow in the position I found it, and deliberately gazed about the room. I observed every facet about the space, burning the vision deep into my memory. I feared I may never see this spot again and I wanted to make sure, whatever happened, I could draw upon this memory to bring me solace and rid me of my fear. In this room I was safe, and so I wanted to bring the room with me, if only in my heart and mind.

I calmly bid farewell to the room, my parents, and my grandmother. I thanked them for being with me, giving me the strength and support to do what must be done, and turned to leave. As I headed toward the stairs, I saw out of the corner of my eye, the rocking chair move of its own accord and once again heard the beautiful voice of my grandmother as she began the song again.

Chapter 34

Paul and Dave avoided the precinct as if it contained victims of the plague. With the headline announcing the death of a prominent citizen and highlighting the fact that the police were looking for an exorcist, made spending any time in the bullpen a living hell. Every cop had to have their poke at the bear. Their brethren were brutal; telling jokes, making snide comments and just being a pain in the ass. It was impossible to get any serious work done in such a hostile environment, so they closeted themselves in the war room. It was also a good way to stay out of sight of the Brass who were looking for the two detectives, and not in a good way.

"So now what do we do?" lamented Paul to the older seasoned detective.

Dave gave no answer. He just sat on the old upholstered chair and stared into space. If he was thinking, sleeping or daydreaming, Paul had no idea. Paul hurled an empty beer bottle directly at him. He handily caught it and dropped it on the floor at his feet without blinking. He resumed his pose and Paul just sighed. Eventually, he got up from the chair and walked over to the board in the middle of the room. The board contained, in excruciating detail, everything they knew about the murders so far, which was not enough. Photos, descriptions of the crimes and what minimal data they had were linked using red string in an attempt to link information with the hope of arriving at a conclusion, or at least an idea. Dave stood there stroking his chin, pacing from one side of the board to the other, finally exclaiming, "I got nothing. If these crimes were committed by a person, then that person is the best serial murderer in history. No clues. No trace.

Nothing to go on whatsoever." He flopped back into the chair.

"Okay," Paul said, "you brought it up first, so let's say it out loud. Could our unsub be something not human?"

"Stupid as it sounds, that's the best I can come up with. Look, we have gone over the scenes with a fine-tooth comb. The murders seem to be unrelated, except for location. All were committed in and around Westons Mills. Other than that, there is no tie in whatsoever."

"Okay, okay, good. We have a tie in. Location. That's the clue. There is something about the location that ties this all together." Paul jumped up excitedly as if a light went off in his head. So, what do we know about Westons Mills area?"

"Well," said Dave, "it is an unincorporated community bordering East Brunswick and New Brunswick. Nothing unusual there."

'Okay, good. What else do we know?" Paul continued grasping at straws.

"On the north end there is the Raritan River, with a tributary off shoot called Lawrence Brook. Part of the brook is dammed off forming Westons Mill pond which feeds the local reservoir which is used for drinking water."

"Then it is surrounded on three sides by water, right?" Paul said.

"So?"

"I don't know, I heard somewhere that water is a source of energy for supernatural manifestations."

"Jesus, now you are sounding like one of those crazy guys on TV chasing ghosts." retorted Dave.

"Hey, you brought it up in the first place. I'm just saying it makes sense. Look, if you have a better idea I am all ears." Just then the phone rang, with Dave saying, "Saved by the bell!" He reached over and hit the speakerphone so both he and Paul would hear. "Hello."

"I just found a way to get to an exorcist." Dr. Howell exclaimed," I have a friend in the priest business who is really a great guy and quite progressive when it comes to fringe thinking. He's having a retirement party tomorrow night at Tabor house and we must go. Maybe he can tell us how to find an exorcist. Whatta ya think?"

Dave said, "Are you actually saying you really want to pursue the concept that this is not natural. In fact, you want to really call this supernatural and look for an exorcist? Really, is that what we have come to."

Without hesitation, she said, "Yes, that is exactly what I am saying."

"Jesus, Emily, I'm not sure I really want to go down that road. I know it was my idea and I really regret that now, but is that really what we should do, get an exorcist? Really? "

"Dave, look. We have gone over this from one end to the other. We have nothing to go on. Maybe if we speak with

159

someone who is on the outside fringe we can see something we don't see right now. Maybe, just maybe, we just might find the clue that ties this all together. I am a scientist, I only believe what I can see and test and prove. I don't see anything, can't test anything and I have no proof of anything. I don't like it any more than you do, but what the hell, nothing ventured nothing gained, right? "

Paul finally spoke up. "Dave, I have to agree with Dr. Howell on this one. We have nothing to lose. Maybe the priest will tell us we are indeed crazy thinking this is supernatural, maybe he will see something we don't. There is nothing to lose, besides there will be free food and drink, right?" He forced a smile.

Breathing a deep sigh, Dave relented. "Okay, okay, I am outnumbered. Tomorrow we head over to Tabor house, talk to your friend and see what we do next. Agreed?"

Paul and Emily replied in unison, "Agreed."

Chapter 35

The next evening, Paul and Dave met Emily just outside of Tabor House, located just off Nichol Ave. on the Douglass College Campus. The ministry serves the student body of the University and many of the locals. Tabor House is known as a welcoming place where the mind and the spirit can experience true peace. The ministry is run by the most affable Father William "Bill" Mickiewicz.

The detectives were dressed casually in slacks and button-down shirts out of respect for the occasion. They left all the accoutrements of their profession, gun badge etc. at home. This visit was off book, way off book. Dave was a little stunned when he caught sight of Emily. Seeing her for the first time without the covering of a lab coat, he gave a little gasp as he felt his heart leap into his throat. She was stunning.

Emily was dressed in a tight-fitting skirt and loose-fitting blouse, the combination of which really showed off her figure. On her feet were a casual pair of shoes with a slight heel that tightened her legs enough to show just how well muscled they were. She approached the detectives. "Wow, you two clean up well."

Dave was tongue tied, but Paul said, "You don't look too bad yourself."

"I'll take that as a compliment. "

Dave replied, "You should," while making a gesture to

161

Emily to lead the way to the front door at Tabor House. Dave continued, "Shall we do this?" Emily took the lead with Paul and Dave close behind. Paul made a gesture to Dave affirming his approval of how beautiful Emily looked. Dave nodded in agreement.

"I saw that," Emily called looking over her shoulder, "let's get this party going."

Emily walked up to the front door and saw the ever-present Christogram. Reaching out to knock, the door opened before she could make contact. There was the tinkling sound of a small bell as the door opened.

"Well, now everyone is here," called Father Bill Mickiewicz. "And who are these fine-looking gentlemen?"

"Father Bill, it's so good to see you!" Emily came through the door and grabbed Bill in a bear hug, kissing him first one cheek, then the other, patting his back all at the same time.

Returning the hugs and kisses, Bill said, "And Em, it's so good to see you, as well. Are you still singing?" Turning to Paul and Dave, Bill said, "Did you know that Em here has the finest soprano voice that ever graced the folk choir during her Douglass days?"

Emily blushed. "Father Bill, really, you are really too much. These are my colleagues. May I present Paul Mercuri and Dave Delair." She was careful to leave out the fact they were cops.

"Gentlemen. It's a pleasure to meet you." Father Bill shook their hands. "Please do come in, enjoy the fun and by all means have a drink. I know I will." Bill held Dave by the hand and led him into the room, all the while telling him how beautiful a voice Emily possessed.

Paul looked at Emily and jokingly said, "This could be fun." He followed Bill and Dave to the bar. Emily shook her head a little and followed Paul.

Soon all four of them had a drink in hand and Bill was regaling some of Emily's exploits from her college days. They were laughing, drinking and having a grand old time. Emily was a little embarrassed by all the attention Bill was giving her. It was as if Bill were trying to pair her off. She, finally said, "Father Bill, I have to admit, we came here for an ulterior purpose."

"Well, do tell," said Father, in a whimsical tone, while taking another pull on his fresh glass of Macallan.

Taking a deep breath, Emily continued, "We need your help. Do you know anyone who might, well, kind of, know someone who might know someone who could be an exorcist?"

"An exorcist! Well, well my dear, what have you gotten yourself into?" He lowered his voice, adding to the conspiratorial tone. "I hope you're not in any danger?"

"No, no of course not, but, Father, this is really hard to talk about. As you know, I work in the medical examiner's office and we have run into a case, several cases, actually, that well, seem a little outside the normal."

"I see." Bill put his glass down on the tray and assumed a priestly stature. "Does this have anything to do with the current spectacle of murders, which, recently, culminated in the brutal death of The Colonel?"

It was Dave who replied, "Yes sir, it does. You see, Paul and I are New Brunswick detectives working the case, and well, we just have run up against a wall, and we, well, just wanted to explore another line of investigation."

"Well, that is indeed interesting."

"Interesting, Father?" Paul said. "What do you mean?"

"Well, yesterday I was talking with a colleague, who, shall we say has some special interests in the supernatural. He expressed a specific interest in this case."

Emily, Dave and Paul exchanged confused looks. "I don't understand," commented Emily. "Why would a colleague be interested in this case?"

"Well, perhaps, you can ask him yourself," stated Father, indicating with a head nod at a priest standing near the stairs. "He's right over there. Perhaps an introduction is in order?"

Chapter 36

The four walked over toward a young man dressed in a fine black suit with a Roman collar. He was standing alone, as if he were waiting for them. As they got closer they could see that he was impossibly handsome. Tall, lean with fine European features and a full head of very dark hair. As the four approached, the young man stepped forward to greet them.

Father Bill said, "This fine young man is my secretary; Father James Donovan, but he prefers to be called Jimmy. Only heaven knows why."

Jimmy shook the hand of each as Father Bill introduced them. When the introductions were complete, Bill continued, "Emily here tells me she has a situation that is more in your area of expertise than mine. It seems she and her friends are looking for an exorcist."

"Well, that is interesting," said Father Jim, in a voice that was strong, yet sympathetic.

"Yes, it is, I shall leave them in your capable hands."

Father Bill gave Emily another hug and whispered, "May the protection of the Lord be with you and your friends. I ask St. Michael, and all of the angels, to protect and watch over you and your friends. I ask this in the name of the Father, the Son and the Holy Spirit. Amen." With this he kissed each cheek, and, in a sympathetic voice, said, "I hope Jimmy here can be of some help."

Turning toward Paul and Dave, Bill shook their hands and gave each of them a similar blessing. Holding Dave's hand a little longer, Father Bill said, "Please take care of Em, she is one of the best." He smiled and walked away.

Before another tick of the clock, Farther Jim said, "Shall we go to my study, where we can discuss the matter undisturbed?" Without waiting for a reply, Jimmy started up the stairs.

Emily followed. Dave was close behind with Paul picking up the rear. They had no idea what was about to happen. If they did, they would have never climbed those stairs.

Chapter 37

As they climbed the stairs, they noticed that the noise of the party below suddenly quieted down to a point where one could not tell a party was in play. The party was still in full swing, but the noise had simply abated. Emily commented to Paul, "Did it just get quiet in here?"

Paul whispered, "Yup, strange huh?"

Father Jim, having reached the top of the stairs, turned and said, "It is always much quieter up here, perhaps because we are closer to heaven!" Chuckling, he bid the trio follow him down the hall and into the last room on the right.

Opening the unlocked door, Farther Jim stood aside to allow his guests to enter first. "Please forgive the lack of ambiance to the room. I am just a poor parish priest," he called, following them into the study.

For a 'poor parish priest' the room was welcoming yet modestly appointed. There was a large throw rug in the center of the room that added a panoply of colors. There was a couch and three armchairs arranged around the colorful rug in sort of a conversation pit arrangement.

There were two table lamps designed to add a warm glow to the atmosphere. In the center was a coffee table replete with Bible, several notepads with various notes written in a flowing style, and a candy dish filled with jelly beans. The room smelled of roses.

Father noted the jelly beans and said, "I am afraid it is my weakness. I adore them and always have some available for temptation."

The couch was well worn and very comfortable. Emily sat down, then fixed her skirt so as not to show too much leg and reached for a jelly bean. "I am afraid we share the same temptations, Father." They all chuckled a little allowing the climate in the room a chance to relieve some of the stress that was building.

Father Jim motioned to Paul and Dave and said, "Please, sit, make yourselves comfortable. May I get you something to drink? We always have a supply of Macallan in the house. Father Bill enjoys a nip or two when working, it settles his nerves." Father Jim was standing at the dry sink that doubled as a bar and offered a glass to his guests.

"You know Father, I think before this night is through we are all going to need a nip or two, so yes, a round for the house, if you please," offered Dave, settling into a very comfortable armchair.

"Sounds good," added Paul.

"I'm in," Emily said.

"Well, then great," replied Father, pouring a healthy shot into their four glasses. He added an ice cube to each, commenting that "a good single malt Scotch requires a little water to breath and bring out the flavor of the oak barrel." The ice cracked as it hit the warm amber liquid. "The sound of heaven opening the gates," chided Father, the ice cracking once for each glass. The trio offered a nervous a laugh, as they looked at each other.

Father Jim handed out the glasses and proceed to take up a position in the open arm chair. He swirled his drink for a moment, breathing in the spirit. He then broke the silence, "So, tell me why you are interested in an exorcist?"

Chapter 38

Father's question just hung there like the proverbial elephant in the room. No one spoke. No one stirred. The only sound came from Father's glass as he swirled the ice cubes round and round, the clinking of the ice began to weigh heavily on their overwrought nerves.

Emily was the first to speak, or at least, try. 'Well, ah, well you see, we have an, well an issue." It was painfully obvious she had lost her nerve. Asking a priest about finding an exorcist to help with a criminal case just seemed absurd. She wiggled on the couch, uncomfortable with being in the spotlight. She took a long pull at the liquid, as she tried to go on. It was obvious she was out of her comfort zone. She turned toward Dave for help.

Dave nodded to Emily as he began to give voice to their predicament. "You see, Father Jim, we are all working on a case, a case that is very high profile and, well, we just don't have a direction. There are things we can't explain. We just don't know." Realizing he was making no sense, Dave sat back in his chair and said, "Sorry, sir, this is much harder than I thought." Dave leaned back into the chair and dropped his shoulders as if in defeat. He just didn't have the nerve or words to elucidate their situation properly. He drained the glass of Macallan then put it on the coffee table.

Father rose from his chair and looked directly at Dave. "I see." He picked up the empty glass, heading to the dry sink to replenish the liquid. He turned toward Paul, who was doing his best to shrink into the upholstery of the chair.

"Perhaps you could shed some light on the situation at hand, young man."

Paul just sat there silently. He could not formulate a response that would make any more sense than Emily or Dave tried to do, so he decided the better part of valor was silence.

"Ok then, perhaps I can assist, "offered Father, filling the glass. He added the required ice cube, returned the glass to Dave, then turned to look directly at the triumvirate before him. His face was calm as was his stature. He was prepared to wait all night if that is what it took to help these people. Calmly he walked back to his chair. He put his glass down on the coaster on the table to his right. He sat back and crossed his legs in a most peculiar manner with his right leg folded completely over his left knee. Carefully he pressed the crease of his trousers to remove any hint of a wrinkle. He then sat slightly forward and precisely folded his hands in a very strange manner. First, he crossed his last three fingers, while keeping his index fingers pointed up; he then crossed his thumbs. Before speaking, he placed his index fingers just under his chin and in a lecturing tone began, "It seems to me that you three are working in tandem on a high-profile case that involves several murders, the latest of which involves one of our fair city's most renowned citizens. The case is baffling, due to the fact that there are no immediate suspects, no apparent connections between the victims and, most puzzling of all, there are no clues, no trace and an ever-escalating horror to the nature of the crimes. How am I doing so far?" He sat back in the chair waiting for a response from his guests.

Emily, Dave and Paul shared horrified glances. It was obvious that 'Jimmy' knew much more than they thought. In fact, he knew everything.

Dave sat up straight, wearing a scowl. "How do you know all this?"

"Suffice it to say," he said, "I have a colleague that is very interested in this case. He possesses, shall we say, some special qualities, in that he has the ability to gather information from sources one might not normally access for information. He is unique among his peers. In fact, it was fortuitous that you three should come here tonight seeking council. I have been given to understand that my associate would like to meet with you to explore some concepts he has that might bring about a solution to the current situation, but he was concerned about reaching out directly." Father sat back and took a long refreshing pull from the remaining Macallan, draining the balance of the amber liquid. "Would anyone like a refresher?" He rose from the chair and proceeded to pour himself another serving.

Emily, Dave and Paul just sat there, stunned. Neither knew what to say or do. Father had a 'colleague with unique abilities' with an interest in this case? How could that be? Except for some recent bad press, when it was revealed the police were looking for an exorcist, nothing about the details of the case were known to the public. Yet, here, simple Father Jimmy, knew everything. The details he presented were spot on. No one outside the three of them knew all that Father just revealed. Perhaps Father Jimmy was not so simple at all. And who was this associate and how could he know as much as he was presented to know.

The triune was lost in thought when finally, it was Emily who broke the silence, "Father," Emily said, "everything you said is true. The nature of the crimes is indeed escalating to proportions that seem outside the natural boundary of what is possible."

"So then, if we continue that line of thought, it would lead us in a direction that would be supernatural."

"Yes sir, that is exactly why we are here tonight," added Paul. "We have come here to seek advice on how we might approach this case from a supernatural point of view. We discussed the options and concluded that this approach to the situation was more in your line of work than ours."

"Well, then, let us proceed along those lines, shall we?" replied Father returning to his chair with a fresh glass of scotch. "Before we go any further, you must accept and agree that once we go through that door, there is no turning back. Once we leave the comfort of the natural world and enter the realm of the spiritual, we are dealing with forces that do not always obey the laws of the natural order. It may be required to do some things that on the surface appear to be wrong, or impossible, but I assure you, everything that needs to be done will have been well thought out and designed to preserve the natural order of things." He stopped talking and looked at each of them for a moment. His face was now solemn, serious. It was as if he had taken on a new persona, one that was all knowing. He seemed to peer into their eyes, perhaps into their very souls seeking a response.

"There are forces, entities, that, if unleashed, can wreak havoc on our world. You must be prepared for what may happen and must accept the possibility that certain actions may need to be taken that are contrary to what would normally feel comfortable." Again, he paused looking at each of them. "Are you sure you are willing to go down such a path?" He sat back, folded his hands once again in that peculiar manner, and waited for their reply.

Dave said, "Sir, I have been a cop all my professional career. I have seen the horrible underbelly of society. I have seen the cruelty that one man can deliver to another. What I have seen here makes all that look like a walk in the park. We have applied all the scientific and theoretical studies we can muster to crack this case. The recent murder was committed by something not of this world. So yes, sir, in response to your query we are indeed committed to go through that door."

Although silent, both Emily and Paul nodded in agreement.

"In that case, I would ask of you an accommodation. My colleague keeps a very peculiar schedule. I would ask that you think this over carefully and, if by tomorrow night, you are all still in agreement, you are to proceed, and return here, to Tabor House, precisely at midnight. My colleague will be waiting. I will pray for you and your souls and ask for God's protection and help in your quest to stop this menace by whatever means necessary."

Emily, Dave and Paul exchanged glances, nodding. "Father," Emily said, "we thank you for your time and appreciate your help and guidance. I am sure we will return tomorrow as per your directions and together we will find the answers we seek."

With this said Emily rose and shook Father's hand, then gave him a warm embrace. Stepping back from her embrace, Father then shook hands with the detectives, wishing them well. He provided a short blessing saying; "Discretion will protect you, and understanding will guard you." He completed the blessing with a sign of the cross made on their forehead and bid them good night.

They left the study and proceeded downstairs. The house was silent, the guests having retired from the party. There was a small light lit in the room down the hall. Emily recalled that this was Father Bill's library.

She had spent many an evening with Father and different discussion groups in this room. She recalled the well-worn yet comfortable chairs, the few books on the shelves and the love within gave her comfort. From out of the darkness of the unlit hall, came the pleasant voice of Father Bill, "Goodnight Emily, may the peace of the Lord be with you always."

"And also, with you," came her rote reply.

They exited Tabor House and stood for a moment on the stoop. "Well, that just happened!" offered Emily with a little fear in her voice.

"I don't know, but if I was a betting man I would say this was a set up. They knew we were coming and they knew what we needed before we said a word."

Paul continued Dave's though by adding, "I'm not sure if we were seeking help from them or they were seeking help from us. Either way, we are in it now, together.

What happens next is anyone's guess."

"Agreed," Emily said. "Until tomorrow?"

Dave and Paul replied in unison, "Until tomorrow." Emily bid the pair farewell by saying, "We better get some sleep tonight. I'm guessing from here on, sleep will be a luxury that will be sorely missed." Emily smiled.

How prophetic those words would soon become.

Chapter 39

I returned to the main part of the house and secured the secret panel to the loft. I stood there a moment and wondered, what does one do to prepare for the possibility of death three days hence?

Actually, I had no idea. I headed to my study, a room filled with books of science, to contemplate my next move. I sat at my desk, not bothering to turn on the lights, as it was just twilight. The room was cast in shadows, as was my very soul. I just sat there as the light faded, bringing to an end day one of my wait.

An idea suddenly came to me; being Italian, food was always a way to bring comfort to body and soul. I decided to make a feast of all my favorite foods. Jumping up from the desk chair, I was now a man with a mission. I headed toward the kitchen to prepare a feast for one, thinking it may be my last.

I raided the refrigerator and found meat for meatballs, a chicken breast, which I planned to turn into chicken parmigiana, and a single sausage perfect for sausage and peppers. I rummaged a little longer and pulled out cheeses, pasta sauce, peppers and onions and the first of many beers to come.

Setting everything on the counter, I opened the beer and drained it in one pull. Returning to the refrigerator, I reached for a second. What the heck, live for today for tomorrow we die!

Laughing out loud, I started the meal preparations. Cutting, slicing, mixing and combining the various ingredients into the proper dish configurations, I ate up the better part of two hours preparing my 'last supper.'

As my delicacies were cooking, I opened my third beer and grabbed a slice of fresh Italian bread. I took a small plate from the cabinet. Placing it on the kitchen table, I added olive oil, balsamic vinegar, red roasted pepper, a little salt and ground black pepper, and a healthy helping of parmesan cheese. I mixed this vigorously with my fork, and cleaned the fork with my mouth, delicious. I then dipped the Italian bread into the mixture and bit off a piece. It was as if all my family were present for that bite. I hoisted my beer bottle and made a toast. "To family!" As I finished the last swallow, I swore I heard an echo off to the side: "Alla famiglia." I knew then, I was not alone, my family was with me. I felt at peace.

By 11:00 p.m. I had finished eating my dinner and polished off my last bottle of beer. I was exhausted and happy all at the same time. I cleaned the dishes, wiped the table and put everything back where it belonged. Satisfied, I stood in the kitchen, contemplating my next move. For a moment I thought I would return to the loft to sleep but thought better of it. Once again, I headed to the master bedroom for a much-needed rest.

The next morning, I woke fresh and alert. I had expected a little hangover from the seven beers I consumed last night, but this morning the demons of alcohol were nowhere to be seen. I rose from bed, performed my toilet ritual and dressed for the day.

Now, under normal circumstances, a person who was about to die, may consider saying goodbye to those people who mean something to them. It suddenly dawned on me, I had no one to say goodbye to!

All my family died over a century ago. I had no close friends, or even acquaintances for that matter. No special girl, no BFF. There were some special students, those that excelled in biological sciences, that I befriended, but they soon were gone after graduation as they entered the next phase of their life. So, there was no one. I didn't even have a pet!

Before I descended further into morose thoughts, I decided to head to the lab; at least there I could say goodbye to my life's work. I grabbed my backpack, opened the front door and headed outside.

I felt the sun shining over me, and it felt great. This is what it meant to be alive. With an extra bounce to my step, I jumped down the porch steps two at a time and hit the road toward Thompson Hall. No one was out, I was entirely alone.

In a few minutes, I reached the basement door at Thompson that led directly into that part of the building reserved for scholarly research. I had spent the better part of two decades in this building, over my two lifetimes, and knew that, here, were my only friends. The ghosts and spirits of those who before me worked these very same laboratories. Their discoveries lived forever in the annals of science. Their names were etched on a bronze plaque that proudly hung in the front hall upstairs where all could see and marvel at who came before. Their spirits, haunting the darkened corridors of the basement, whispering inspiration to those who toiled at scientific discovery. I opened the side door and entered the bowels of higher learning.

In my first life, as a graduate student I had completed my master's degree and began working on my doctorate when tragedy struck. A century later, my life returned by Ezerial, I was continuing my work both as a researcher and professor of biology. If these walls could talk!

I proceeded down the hall toward my private lab. As I did, my hand glided lovingly over the tiled walls of the hallway, as if shaking hands with a friend. I was saying goodbye to the building and its inhabitants, both living and dead.

Soon I reached the entrance to my lab and stopped. There on the door was my name: "Dr. R Mauro Professor of Biology/ Department Chair". I traced the painted letters, as if saying goodbye to each individual letter. This was my legacy, this was who I am and perhaps, soon enough, who I was.

After my brief reverie, I entered the lab to find it in perfect order. I was not one of those mad scientists that kept a cluttered lab, papers scattered about, white boards filled with calculations and theories, test tubes scattered helter skelter. No, my lab was neat and tidy.

As I walked around just looking at the contents of my shelves, I reached out and pulled down a dusty old black bound master's thesis. It was hidden behind some papers I had stacked up so that no one would find it. It was my original work from 1918! The work was entitled, *Serotypical Analysis of Avian Infectious Bronchitis Virus*. I brushed off the layer of dust and opened to the signature page. There were the names of my committee, my friends. As I read their names, Dr. John Grun, Dr. Eugene Adams and Dr. Rex Gilbreath, my heart was filled with the memories of a time when there was so much ahead of me, and I was happy. As happy then as I am now, reliving the memory. I read through the manuscript, for old times' sake, and replaced it on the shelf. Once again, I stacked the papers in front to hide it from view. Satisfied, I turned a full circle around the lab and just took in all the sights, smells and memories I could muster. My heart and soul were now at rest. I was ready to say goodbye to these, my many friends, and move on.

I locked the door when suddenly I heard some footsteps down the hall to my right. I looked in the direction of the sounds. I called out "goodbye old friends, I hope to see you on the other side, if that is my fate." Hearing no reply save the echo down the hall, I turned and climbed the stairs back out into the fading sunlight. And so, my second day was coming to a close.

I headed home and prepared a light meal, partially from last night's leftovers and partly a new addition of pasta, I settled in for the night. After dinner, I retired to the den and decided to finish the book I was reading, a story from Dan Brown called *Origin*. I just had to know how it ended, so I would finish the book and head to bed.

All too soon, the sun rose, ushering in the dawn of the third and final day. I had no special plans. My book complete, my goodbyes said, I was ready to face whatever was destined to befall me. My mind, my body, and my heart were ready for whatever was to come. I spent this final day in my study, alone with my thoughts.

Raised as a good Catholic boy, I decided late in the afternoon that perhaps I should consider some form of prayer as I prepared my soul for the battle ahead. Not one to have bent the knee in prayer for a very long time, I really didn't know how or where to begin. I didn't have any religious icons in the house nor even the required crucifix hung in a place of prominence. No rosary, not even a Bible. *Some Catholic you are*, I thought.

Not seeing any other options, I decided the best I could do was to go into the living room where there was a large picture window that faced the setting sun. I opened the curtains and let in the evening colors: red, yellow, and blue bedazzle the room as the sun fell further below the horizon. I decided here was the best place to offer my prayer.

I fell on my knees, made the sign of the cross and prayed aloud, "Dear Lord, giver of life, I thank thee from my heart for the gifts you have given me. For my family, my friends, my second life I thank you. I shall not lie to you, for I am afraid, afraid of what is to come. What am I to do, Lord? I have not the strength alone to take on this task, to die, to stop a demon and then return to this my life.

Dear Lord, I am calling upon you today for your divine guidance and help. I am in crisis and need a supporting hand to keep me on the right and just path. My heart is troubled, but I will strive to keep it set on you, as your infinite wisdom will show me the right way to a just and right resolution.

Finally, please give your servant, Ezerial, the strength he will need to help and guide me in this, my trial, ahead. I beseech you for strength and for wisdom that I would be able to endure this situation and be able to handle it in a way that will close the rift between worlds and brings peace and harmony back into this world. Amen"

I was as ready now as I would ever be. There was nothing to do now but wait, and so I waited, alone with my thoughts.

Chapter 40

It was a beautiful clear August evening. The moon was almost full and playing peek- a- boo behind some wisps of clouds. The air was fresh with the scent of Amaryllis wafting down from the campus greenhouse. I was thinking it was a beautiful evening to be alive as I left the house on Seamen Street for the walk over to Tabor House and my meeting with Ezerial. Yes, it was a beautiful evening to be alive and now I wondered how much longer I would be alive; as Ezerial's plan to deal with Shingas included my imminent death. I shuddered as I made my way down the street, along Nichol Ave. on toward Tabor House.

I arrived a few minutes before midnight and proceeded up the stairs to the front door. I knew the door would be unlocked so I let myself in. As always, the foyer was very dimly lit, as the only light came from the library down the hall. As I turned toward my left, I started to head toward the library, and my fate, when I heard Ezerial call out, "Please show our guests to the library. I shall be there momentarily."

Guests! What guests? We never had any guests during our discussions! Before I could call out to ask what was going on, I heard a soft knock on the front door. I hesitated for a split second and took a deep breath to steel myself for what was to come. I let it out slowly and reached out to open the door and greet our "guests."

I was somewhat stunned to see, standing at the entrance to Tabor house, three people. One, a very pretty, young lady and two handsome men, one a little older, both with the air of authority. All were dressed casually, as was I.

"Good evening," I said. "Do please come in." I stepped back from the door, opening it to allow our guests entry.

As the three entered, the older gentleman asked, "Wasn't there a bell on the door last night? Strange, but I didn't hear a bell when you opened the door."

An odd comment I thought. "I am not sure I have ever heard a bell before," I lied. I did hear a bell once at this door. It was the only time I came here that was not "at the stroke of midnight." As I recall, I had come that early evening to rail against Ezerial for leaving me, no abandoning me, at the hospital. Instead of meeting with Ezerial, I was introduced to the strange, yet oddly familiar, Father Jimmy Donovan. I did hear a bell then, but never before or since. Strange, I thought, why did these strangers expect to hear a bell. Had they been here before? I was confused but tried not to telegraph my concerns.

The three of us stood there a moment, uncomfortable in not knowing what to do next. The young lady broke the ice, saying, "My name is Dr. Emily Howell, and these are my friends Detectives Dave Delair and Paul Mercuri. We are here to meet with Father Donovan."

That is the second time I heard that name. I was growing more and more confused. Before I could say anything, Ezerial called again from down the hall, "Robbie, please, show our guests to the library. All will be made clear in a minute. Please bid them welcome." I swept my hand toward the library. "Please, right this way. Welcome to Tabor House."

The trio exchanged glances and stood as if rooted to the spot. "Please, follow me. I am sure we can clear this up in the library," I offered, as I tried to follow Ezerial's directive. I didn't wait for a reply but proceeded to lead them toward the library. I didn't look back, assuming they would follow; fortunately, they did.

Ezerial had prepared the library for our guests. The chairs were moved from their normal positions and formed a circle, as if a discussion group were to be held. As we entered the room, I noticed Dr. Howell stopped short of the entry. She had a strange look on her face. She studied the bookcases lining the three walls filled with the immense number of volumes.

"I have been in this room many times when I was a student here," she said. "Father Bill held discussions, and sing-alongs in this very room. I never saw this number of books and fine furniture. How does a simple college minister afford such a fine well stocked library?"

Just then Ezerial made his entrance, "I am sure you are correct, Dr. Howell. All is not always as it seems. Please, please, do all come in, make yourselves comfortable, there is much to discuss and precious little time to do so."

Ezerial stood fully erect, dressed as always in a fine hand-tailored black suit, tonight replete with a black shirt and black tie. He looked as something out of a GQ magazine. Tall, handsome, impeccably dressed, his deep black hair stood in waves upon his head. He was indeed a sight to behold. Once again, he bid them sit down, but no one moved. I saw a frown cross his visage.

"Ah, Father? I, ah, we were expecting Father Donovan. Will he be joining us tonight?" Emily said.

"No, no, I'm afraid not. Father Donovan briefed me on your concerns and I agreed to meet with you. I am Ezerial D'Angelo, but you can call me Ezerial. Please, I beg you do come in, sit. I am sure all will become clear," he said in his most charming manner. It worked. Our guests entered the room and sat, while Ezerial and I remained standing. Ezerial continued, "I would like to introduce my associate, Dr. Robbie Mauro. And, I believe you are Dr. Emily Howell, Detective David Delair and Detective Paul Mercuri of the New Brunswick police?"

Our guests once again exchanged glances. It was Dave who said, "I see you are well versed in who we are, but I am somewhat put out as to who you are, and why Father Donovan will not be here this evening."

"I assure you, all will become clear," replied Ezerial as he took up his seat and bid me do the same. Continuing he said, "Father Donovan indicated that you were looking for advice on finding an exorcist. Is that correct?"

It was Paul who found his voice. "Yes, that's right, are you an exorcist?"

Allowing a small chuckle to escape, Ezerial commented, "Yes, I am indeed an exorcist, and, much more. I do understand your plight, as explained by Father Jimmy, and I am afraid to say, that, after careful consideration, you are not exactly in need of an exorcist."

187

"What, what do you mean?" exclaimed Emily, lunging forward. "We came here to find an exorcist and now you're telling us that is not what we need! What exactly are we doing here?"

"I am sorry if I upset you. We are all here for the same reason. There is something happening; something that cannot be explained by the natural order of things. You have come here to find a solution. I am here to provide one. I am just saying that the solution does not include the duties of an exorcist."

Visibly confused, but calmed down, Emily sat back in her seat. She breathed in a deep sigh. "So, then what do we need?"

Ignoring the question, Ezerial asked one of his own. "Before we continue I must ask each of you, did you come here of your own free will?"

Dave sat forward and retorted, "What does that have to do with anything?"

"Please, allow me a concession. Before we proceed, I must ask you to have a little faith. Faith is what we will need to see this through to the end. I assure you, I want to help. I know I can help, but, humor me if you would, for just a moment. Indulge me in this line, and I assure you, all will be understood. So again, I ask each of you, are you here of your own free will?"

Paul was the first to respond. 'Yes, I suppose so. What other reason would we be here? Yes, to your question."

"Good"

"I agree as well. I am here of my own free will," replied Emily still confused as to the need for the question.

When Dave, however, did not readily respond, Ezerial said, "Detective, I see you are not prepared to answer. Perhaps you will allow me a little latitude?"

"Go on."

"By coming here, you have embarked on a journey that few have chosen, let alone followed to the end. You are a man of power and authority, firmly set in the natural world where things can be seen, touched, examined and understood. You have seen horrors and evil, but you have been able to reconcile those events to the natural laws through your detective skills. You have solved cases that seemed impossible; yet, each and every one of these crimes were perpetrated by a natural, flesh and blood being. Now, it is different. Now your intellect, your experience, your very soul, tells you that there is something happening, something taking place that is outside the natural order and thus you have come here, to explore the supernatural possibilities for a solution to your plight. I need to know, before we go through to that place, that you have come here of your own free will. So, I ask you once again, have you come here of your own free will?"

Dave looked at the others, cleared his throat and said, "Yes, I am here of my own free will."

"Good, then let us proceed."

Chapter 41

The atmosphere in the room became more relaxed. The confusion, seemed to have dissipated, as the adrenalin flushed out of our bodies. Emily and Paul appeared more accepting of what Ezerial said, as they relaxed deeper into their seats. Only Dave was still a little cautious, perhaps not yet fully prepared to trust our host. He remained at the edge of his seat, his face a little taut, staring directly at Ezerial. Ezerial sensed his mood and proceeded to explain in more detail why an exorcist would not be required.

"First, let me disabuse you of the notion that this issue will be resolved through the efforts of an exorcist." Ezerial got up and headed toward the extensive library. Reaching for a thin book, bound in simple skin, he proceed, "I am holding in my hands a copy of The *Roman Ritual* or *Rituale Romanum,* which is one of the official ritual works of the Roman Rite of the Catholic Church. It contains all of the services which may be performed by a priest or deacon, which are not contained within either the *Missale Romanum* or the *Breviarium Romanum*. Within these pages is contained the sacred Rite of Exorcism. It tells us under what conditions an exorcism may or may not be performed and contains the specific prayers and rituals one needs to perform a proper exorcism."

The trio exchanged glances. I too was very interested in where Ezerial was headed, since it somehow involved my death.

Opening the book to the preface he began to read, "The sacred Rite of Exorcism can be traced back to Jesus Christ himself, who performed the first exorcism." Stepping closer to the group, he continued, "It is only a priest, or higher designate, approved by the church, trained in the ritual, who can perform an exorcism. The purpose of an exorcism is to drive out the devil, or one of his minion demons, from a person, or place. In some rare cases, the demon or minion may possess an object from which the exorcist must cast out the evil. The exorcist must prove beyond all doubt, that a possession of a person, place or object has taken place. Before an exorcism can be performed, the exorcist must rule out medical, psychological, physical or hysterical causes for the alleged possession. The Church must rule only after exhaustive analysis, and proof positive, that possession is the only source of the affliction. Under no circumstances may an exorcism be performed without approval from the church, or local bishop, and then, only may be performed by an official designated exorcist."

Placing the tome on the table, he continued, "As you can see we have not begun to meet the requirements to allow the intervention of an exorcism, as we have no person, place or object, proven positively under the requirements of the church, to be possessed; nor do we have approval or authority from the Church to proceed. Further, I contend we are not dealing with Satan or one of his minions, but in fact are dealing with something that could potentially be much worse."

This last comment shocked everyone in the room. Wide-eyed, Paul exclaimed, "What can be worse than the devil?"

Ezerial returned to his seat and once again performed his peculiar ritual. He sat down in the chair, both feet on the floor his body erect. He then folded his right leg completely over his left knee letting the leg dangle. He smoothed the crease of his pant leg to a razor-sharp edge. His then folded his hands such that the last three fingers folded over leaving his index fingers pointed upward. He then put his index fingers under his chin. Addressing the room, he began, "The devil, or Satan, as you know him, can be driven out of a person or place through the power and authority of Mother Church. The devil has a fear of, and is duty bound, to obey the Almighty. He may resist. He may torture and torment a human. But in the end, he must obey and relinquish his hold on the person, place or thing. An exorcist has dominion over the devil, a power given to him directly from our Lord. The prayers invoked by the exorcist have the power of the Almighty. It is only through the word of God himself that Satan can be driven out. What we are dealing with here is not the devil or even a demon. We are dealing with something utterly different; so different that the power of the church has no demonstrable authority to drive the evil from this realm."

The room was silent. You could hear your own heartbeat bracketed by the deep breathing of the others in the room. There was a palpable tension. No one moved. I couldn't stand it any longer I had to break the silence before I went mad. "Well, if an exorcism is not the solution, then what is?"

"That, my dear friend, is where you come in."

Chapter 42

Dr. Howell spoke up. "I'm confused. Last night we met with Father Donovan, and discussed our situation, and he assured me he knew a colleague, an exorcist, who would help us. Now you tell me that an exorcism is useless, yet you have no solution." Her distress was evident in her voice.

"I understand your frustration," Ezerial offered in his most soothing tone. "I assure you that I am indeed an exorcist; and so much more. You must have patience."

Dave jumped up and started pacing. "Patience, sir, is something we no longer have the luxury to enjoy. People are dying out there, and so far, we are powerless to stop it. Who are you to tell us what it is we need and what we don't? We don't know you. We came here at the behest of Father Donovan and he is not even here to vouch for you. As a detective my radar is turned up, way up. I ask you directly, who are you and why should we trust you in the first place?"
"I am Ezerial, a member of the ancient order of Watchers."

"Watchers?" the three said in unison.

Ezerial nodded. "Angels sent down by God Himself to watch over and protect man. I have been since the beginning of time; and I shall be here until the end of time,"

"This is ridic---" Emily spurted, only to be interrupted by Ezerial's continued explanation.

Ezerial replied in a voice soft yet powerful enough to reach to my very soul. "You have come to my house to seek aid in

193

dealing with the unknown and unknowable. Your search has brought you here of your own free will. I will help you in this quest, but it is you who must learn and accept that which is not seen, and do that which must be done, to stop this evil before the veil between the darkness and the light is irreparably torn and that evil on a grand scale is allowed entry into this time and place. I may be your only hope, so either trust me or all is lost."

This was followed by silence.

It was my time to speak. "I know what you must be thinking. The man is mad. I assure you, he is not. He is all that he says he is, and more, much more. Ezerial saved me from death, a death that had taken hold of me a long time ago. I didn't believe in him at the start either. He opened my eyes to things that I would never have believed were true had I not seen them myself. There is a spiritual realm that is just beyond the veil. We cannot see it, but, it is there. There is a parallel time and space, beyond our comprehension. We are allowed to see an infinitesimal percentage of the entire universe. Suffice it to say, what is really out there is well beyond the comprehension of even the highest intellect man can muster. Ezerial is indeed a Watcher, an angel of the Lord. Give him the chance, and I assure you, he will resolve this situation. If you do not, there may be no hope, and all will be lost. What is coming is coming, unless we stop it, here and now. Listen with your hearts, keep your minds open to what is possible. Although it may seem impossible in the beginning, it is the right path. We are all here, in this room, of our own free will. We must work together, to fight this thing, for we are stronger together than alone. Give him a chance." I sat back

194

exhausted, both physically and emotionally. My tirade was followed once again by silence.

Chapter 43

Dave shook his head, "I don't know. I need proof. Something I can touch or see. I may not have the faith in you that seems to be required."

"Fair enough." Ezerial remained seated, he was actively thinking, weighing Dave's words and contemplating what to do next. Finally, after a few moments in which no one hardly breathed, Ezerial spoke again.

"But the Almighty has faith in you, Ezerial said. "Dave, do you remember the summer of your twelfth year?"

"What does that have to do with anything?"

"Indulge me." Before Dave could interrupt, Ezerial continued, "You broke your arm that year, am I right?"

A look of shock crossed Dave's face. Emily and Paul sat back in shock.

"You were a strong-willed child that grew to be a strong-willed man. It is that strength that makes you who you are today. But let's go back to that day, shall we? Please, Dave, tell us what happened."

Dave hesitated, scowling. "I...I climbed a tree in the backyard, the branch broke and I broke my arm. End of story." Dave's reply was somewhat caustic but laced with a little fear.

"Is that the whole story?" Ezerial said, implying there was more.

Dave did not reply, so Ezerial continued, "In fact, Dave, you loved to climb that tree. It was one of your favorite places to go and hide among its leaves and think. You climbed that tree almost every day that summer. On that particular morning, your mother specifically told you not to climb that tree anymore. You were growing heavier, and she feared the branches could no longer support your weight. Isn't that right?"

Silence, followed by a nod.

"But that morning, after breakfast, you left the house and ran to the backyard and climbed that tree, just like every other day. You did this of your own free will. No one was going to tell you what you could or could not do."

"Yes," was all that Dave could say. I saw the blood had left his face. He was ashen and shaken.

"You climbed higher and higher that day, didn't you? You climbed higher than you had ever climbed before, up into the new growth, the taller, weaker branches."

Again, barely a perceptible nod from Dave.

"Suddenly, the branch began to give way. You were nearly thirty feet in the air. There was no time to climb down, was there? You were going to fall, and you instantly knew you could be hurt. Hurt really bad, no?"

Dave fell back deeper into the chair as the memory filled his subconscious, bringing back all the terror he must have felt at that moment, the moment just before he fell.

"Tell us Dave, tell us exactly what happened next"

In a voice that was barely audible Dave said, "I felt the branch breaking. I knew I had to do something, but there was no time. I tried to reach for a lower branch, a stronger branch, but instead I went hurling through the lower branches toward the ground." Dave stopped speaking reliving the moment he began to fall.

Using his most soothing voice, Ezerial urged him, "Go on. What happened next?"

"I fell, but something happened. I could feel myself fall as the branch finally broke. But I didn't fall, well not exactly."

"Tell us Dave, what do you mean? What happened next?"

"I started to fall head first. In the area below the base of the tree was a rock wall. I was heading, head first, into the pile of rocks. I was sure that I was going to die."

"But you didn't, Dave. Why?"

Almost in a trance, Dave continued, "Time around me slowed down. I could see the ground coming at me real fast, then, suddenly, it was as if I was floating. I had time to adjust my trajectory. I was able to kick out, hard, with my right leg. I kicked out just hard enough to hit a big branch, which caused me to fall off to the right of the rock wall. I was also able to turn slightly so that when I hit the ground, it was my arm that struck first and not my head. Then, just as suddenly, I hit the ground and broke my arm."

"What happened next?"

"I screamed in pain, my mother heard me, and she came running. Frantic, she raced back to the house and called an ambulance which came and took me to the hospital."

"When the doctor came to set your arm, and your mother told him the story, what did the doctor say, exactly?"

"He said that I was one lucky young man. If I had hit those rocks with my head, I would surely have died. Someone up there must have a higher purpose for me."

"He does, Dave. He has a higher purpose for you, and it is here and now. You were saved by the hand of the Almighty. You may not have enough faith to believe in Him, but He has enough faith to believe in you. We need you, Dave, we need your strength. Are you willing now, to set your doubt aside and come along freely, and help us stop what is to come?"

Without a moment's hesitation, Dave whispered, "Yes."

Chapter 44

Turning toward Dr. Howell, Ezerial asked, "What do you know of the dead, Doctor?"

Emily startled a moment, you could see her eyes flash wide. She rocked her head back as if from a blow before she was composed enough to respond. "The dead? Well, the dead are... well, dead. I work with them every day in my capacity as a coroner. I don't understand."

"Do you commune with the dead? Do they tell you things?"

"Well, yes, in a way, I guess they do. I use my training as a doctor and a forensic scientist to learn all I can about the deceased. From there, I look to find the root cause of death, and then, hope to determine if a crime was committed. If there was, I delve deeper into the deceased and tease out the story, line by line, until I know how they died. Then, I follow the clues and look for a trail that may lead to their killer. So, my answer is, yes, I do in a way, speak to the dead." She was speaking more to herself than to the room.

"If I were to tell you there is more to the dead than meets the eye, how would you feel?"

"I don't know. I mean, what could you possibly mean?"

"Suffice it to say, that upon the moment of death, there is a release of energy, the energy of life, which some may call the soul. This energy, usually dissipates almost instantaneously. The lifeforce, once so powerful within the living body, is weak and lost upon death, so it returns to the universe, whence it came."

"I can accept that," replied Emily after ample consideration.

"Good then." Ezerial continued, "Let us assume, for a moment, that a very small percentage of those who have died have a much stronger life's energy. Let's say it is strong enough to hold together for a moment or two, perhaps they linger then dissipate."

"Ok that is possible, I suppose."

"Now let us say that an infinitesimally fraction of a percent have a life's energy that is much stronger. Say, their life ended abruptly, or in a manner that was filled with energy, such as hate or fear. Maybe they were strong in life, so strong that they did not want to give up the ghost, as they say, and thus they held onto their life's energy a little bit longer."

"So that could explain poltergeists or ghosts." Emily nodded. "They are residual energy, that, some say, can be measured by special instruments, so I suppose, again, that it may be possible, for a life's energy to linger for a short time."

"What if I told you, that in extreme cases, some powerful souls not only hold onto their energy, but, in fact, they can build upon the energy they possess, by taking from their surroundings, absorbing other sources of energy and increasing their power little by little. Over time, a very long time, they can gather enough energy to interact with the living in such a way that they may be able to take some of the energy from the living for their own needs. In this way, they can grow stronger, until such time, they have built up such a high level of energy, that, they are strong enough to pass through the veil between life and death."

A collective "What!" came from the trio. I remained silent for the story Ezerial just told was much too close to my own story for comfort.

"Impossible," sneered Dave. "Coming back from the dead only happens in the movies."

"Perhaps, perhaps," replied Ezerial, giving Dave his due. "But since we all agreed to pass through the door from the natural to the supernatural, suppose, just suppose for a second, that it is possible, for a dead individual to possess enough energy to crack the door between life and death."

"Ok I will give you that," agreed Dave.

"The best source for the dead to gather energy is from the living. Science has, somewhat reluctantly, accepted the potential for poltergeist activity to have some basis in fact. If the poltergeist can interact with the living, move and object, touch a person, let's say, then it is within the realm of possibilities that a very strong entity, may be able to take the life of a living being and steal its energy. The more horrible the death, the more energy is released, the more the entity can absorb."

The concept hung in the room like a cloud. Suddenly Paul said, "Are you saying that the killer is, in fact, dead himself, and is killing these people to absorb their energy, and thus become strong enough itself to come back from the dead?"

"Precisely."

Chapter 45

Ezerial sat back in the chair and waited, giving the others a moment to absorb what he was saying.

Finally, Emily said, "My God!"

"No, my dear. God has nothing to do with it, but we may call upon Him in the near future to seek His help in resolving what stands before us."

"Well, then what exactly stands before us?" Dave called out.

"A Skadegamutc or Ghost Witch."

"What the hell is that?" Paul said.

Ezerial got up from his chair and walked over to the bookcase, all eyes studying his every move. He reached out and withdrew a battered volume from high up on the shelves. The cover was old and torn, the pages looked fragile. Ezerial carried the book reverently back toward his chair but stopped short of sitting. He turned to his audience and began, "This is the personal diary of one James Somerset, corporeal in the Middlesex County Militia, commanded by Colonel John Neilson." He turned the book so that we could see that it was indeed handwritten and appeared to be authentic.

Everyone was transfixed on Ezerial as he began to read from the diary, "*Today was the most horrible day of my life. I am sure that my soul will be damned in hell forever for what we did this day. Under the orders of Colonel Neilson, we raided an Indian encampment, under the ruse that they were aiding the British and* as such were our enemy as well. *The camp was nestled along the Raritan River a short distance from New Brunswick. We arrived at dawn, and immediately began our attack. The Indians surrendered without hesitation as we approached, as they were not warriors but old men, women and children.*" Ezerial paused for emphasis, then continued, "*The women of the camp began to beg for their lives. The old men fell to their knees, their hands raised, a sign of surrender. The children cried, in fear, from the sight of white men dressed in uniform carrying guns. The battle ended before it began. Colonel Neilson rode up and commanded us "Kill them all down to the last man." The men of our unit turned toward the Colonel in protest, but the Colonel just ordered, "Anyone who does not follow my orders will meet the same fate, now move out!"* Ezerial once again paused. He was clearly distraught, as if this were a personal memory. He cleared his throat and continued, "*The men were horrified at the order, but more afraid of the Colonel if they did not obey. Sargent Somers was the first to act, drawing his sword he plunged it through a wailing squaw who stood crying at his feet. The blood lust began. Soldiers began killing mercilessly using sword, blade and anything they could get their hands on. The Colonel commanded us to save bullets. "These pagans are not worth the cost of a bullet," he screamed over the heads of his murderous men. With a ferocity I have never seen before, the men went about killing every living thing in sight. Babies were dashed against rocks, women were stabbed or strangled. The old men, still upon their knees, were run through or beheaded. The wailing of the dying and the whooping of the soldiers will ring in my ears forever. As the horrors continued, I caught sight of one of the Indian men coming out of his tepee. He was younger than those left in the camp; but was far older than a brave. He was dressed in feathered headdress, long deerskin pants and was painted, not in war paint, but in a fine intricate design that could only be ceremonial.*

Amidst the blood lust, he walked calmly from his tepee and began beating a skin drum and chanting. Facing the sky, he began to dance in a medicine circle. I drew from this he must be the Medicine Man of the tribe. He continued beating his drum, chanting and singing to the sky, beseeching the gods to intervene. He continued to dance and pray, staying far away from the rampage all around him. Colonel Neilson saw the Medicine Man and rode directly at him on horseback.

Turning, the Medicine Man saw Neilson, at full gallop, heading right at him, sword drawn, and knew he was about to die. I heard him cry out, his last words rang in my ears, "I am Shingas and vengeance will be mine!" just before Neilson separated his head from his shoulders.

Soon thereafter, the horrors complete, we returned to our bivouac, covered in blood and gore. I rushed to my tent and threw up. I knew then that what I had witnessed would remain with me for the rest of my life. I will recall the Medicine Man's last words in my sleep: "I am Shingas and vengeance will be mine!"

Ezerial sighed deeply, closed the book and returned it to its home on the shelf. Slowly and deliberately, he sat back in his chair.

Dr. Howell said, "This Shingas, the Medicine Man, are you telling us that he has come back and that is who has been committing these crimes?"

Ezerial merely nodded in assent.

"How do we stop him?" asked Emily.

"We must meet him on his own terms," replied Ezerial solemnly.

"How can we do that, he's dead, right? What can we do to stop a ghost?"

"You can kill my associate, Dr. Mauro," Ezerial replied, matter-of-factly.

Chapter 46

Dave leapt out of his chair. I thought he was going to attack Ezerial, but he showed some restraint. "What the hell, are you crazy!" He stood in front of Ezerial and shouted, "Now I've heard everything! We come here for one concept, you take us for a ride down crazy road and now you want us to sanction murder! Who the hell do you think you are?" Turning away from Ezerial and facing Emily, he reached out a hand to help her out of her chair and said, "Come on, we're getting out of here before something really crazy happens."

Paul rose to his feet and Emily took Dave's hand when I said, "Ezerial is right. The only way for us to stop Shingas is for me to die, again."

Emily looked at me quizzically and fell back into her chair. Dave turned toward me and just stared. Paul was the first to speak, "What the hell do you mean, die again?"

"This is going to be a long story, but suffice it to say, I have been there before."

Dave sat back down. "Okay, Dr. Mauro, you have our attention. Share this long story."

I turned to Ezerial, who smiled encouragingly. I took a deep breath and began. "My name is Dr. Roberto Mauro and I was born in 1893."

"Impossible!" challenged Dave. "That would make you nearly 125 years old! What kind of bullshit story are you slinging?"

"I assure you, it is not BS, as you say, but is the truth. You may feel it is impossible, but I assure you it is true, every word. May I continue?"

Dave made a show of bowing to my request and resumed his seated position. "Ok, big guy, we're all ears."

"As I said, I was born in 1893 in the city of New York. I was raised in the Gravesend section of Brooklyn. When I was a teenager, my two best friends and I came across a very old Ouija or Spirit Board. We had no idea what we were doing. To us it was a game. As kids, we had no idea what danger we could get into, so, we proceeded to play with the board anyway. Our endeavors opened a door to the spirit world that resulted in my death on my twenty-fifth birthday."

Paul interrupted, "If you *died*, then how are you here today?" He looked at as he made the proverbial air quotes with his fingers at the word died.

"I assure you, I did die. In fact, I was dead for a long time. At the time of my death, I was in my prime, my whole life ahead of me. The spirit in the board forecast my death and even told me the exact day I would die, but I ignored her. I suffered a terrible accident. I was not ready to die, and thus, I refused to return my life's energy to the universe. I held it together, growing stronger, until I was able to remain in the place between death and life. I could see the living and feel the dead, but I was not corporeal. I was neither dead nor fully alive." I saw that all eyes were on me. I turned toward Ezerial who once again bid me continue, with a nod of his head. So, I did. I had their undivided attention and kept going with my story.

"There came a time when I was done, I wanted to be released from this time and place. I was prepared to return my energy to the cosmos, but I was interrupted in my plan by the unexpected, a Watcher named Ezerial. He saw through me and made an offer I could not refuse. I could help him on a quest, a quest that was impossible, but if I succeeded, I may be able to regain my corporeal body and continue my life such as it was."

The guests all looked stunned, if not a bit dubious.

"I had nothing to lose and everything to gain, so I followed Ezerial through an extraordinary quest that transcends this time and space, to a parallel universe where we defeated an archangel named Azazel. As a reward for my success, I was able to recover my corporeal body." No one spoke. I could see Emily was processing what I just said. Dave looked at Paul and just shook his head. I don't think I was winning them over.

"Everything Ezerial has told you is absolutely true and I am living proof that the door to the supernatural opens into a realm that is far beyond the capacity of the masses to understand. What is possible, is far beyond your wildest dreams. I am prepared to die, that is, die again, if that's what it takes to defeat this Shingas and put a stop to the horrors that will be unleashed, if he is allowed to tear through the veil between the living and the dead. I am prepared to give my life to the cause, if that is what it takes to put an end to this story." I sat back emotionally exhausted.
Dave clapped his hands three times slowly and said,

"Wonderful story. I give you an A for creativity." Turning to the others, he said, "Come on, it's time to go. I've heard enough." He began to get up when Emily calmly spoke.

"I believe you."

"What!" Dave jumped up. "You can't be serious!"

"I don't know why. I can't begin to articulate a valid reason, but I believe them. What Ezerial said is plausible and Dr. Mauro seems to corroborate the story. I am afraid that if we don't believe them, things could get worse, much worse."

Dave threw up his hands in disbelief. He spun halfway around to look at Paul. "Are you going along with this shit show?"

Paul was silent for a moment, until he said, "Sorry, but I gotta go with Emily on this one. We have no other recourse. We opened this door and agreed that we should follow where it leads. It seems to lead here, so, I guess I'm in."

"Unbelievable!" Dave flopped back down in his chair. "Okay, I'm outvoted, so I guess we see where this goes."

Ezerial smiled and simply said, "Good."

"But wait one minute, Ezerial. If you are such a powerful angel, why can't you just kill Mauro here yourself and bring him back. Why do you need us?" Dave challenged.

"By virtue of my vocation as a Watcher, I am forbidden to interfere in the actions of mankind. As an angel I am

211

forbidden to kill a human being. So, I have two strikes against me."

'Well, what do you call this?" replied Dave spreading his hands and shrugging his shoulders indicating the topic of the discussion. "If this is not interference, then I don't know what is."

"Fair enough, fair enough," responded Ezerial. "In some very special cases, I walk a very tight line between my vocation and what needs to be. You confirmed that you were all here of your own free will. I only told you a story of what is, and what can be. The decision is completely yours. I did not directly interfere, I only provided some information that you were lacking in order for you to make an informed decision."

"Who are you trying to convince with that logic, yourself or me?" retorted Dave.

"God," came the reply. "And I pray He forgives me."

Chapter 47

There was a collective silence in the room, as each person reflected on what they had just heard. I could see that Emily was struggling the most. She was the most religious, although lapsed. I think she wanted to believe all that Ezerial said. However, she was a person of science. She lived in a world where she could see, touch, experiment and develop a course of action based on science, math and analysis. This, life beyond life, was something outside her comfort zone, and I could see it caused her stress.

Dave was hard core, he had witnessed life at its worst, so I doubted he was convinced there was something beyond this life. He dealt with death every day, and no one ever came back from the dead. The dead stay dead and that's it.

Paul was an enigma. He was silent through most of the discussions, a comment here, a question there, but he mostly observed. I couldn't read him very well, so I had no idea what was going on inside his head. So, I sat there silent and waited.

Ezerial had assumed his unnatural pose. Leg folded over, crease in his pant leg smoothed to razor sharp, hands folded in his peculiar way, staring straight ahead. It was as if he made his case as best he could and now he awaited the verdict. If he were concerned, it didn't show. I guess I was nervous enough for the both of us.

Finally, Emily spoke, "So then, what exactly do you want us to do?"

Ezerial breathed a sigh of relief and replied, "We need to enter the realm of Shingas. I have a plan to provide a controlled death for Dr. Mauro. Carried out to perfection, he may be released from this mortal plane and meet Shingas in his own time and space. Robbie must then find a way to stop Shingas. If he is successful in preventing Shingas from crossing over, the veil will once again close. Shingas and the others will be trapped on the other side where they belong. Robbie may have an infinitesimal chance to return to his corporeal body and hopefully resume his mortal life. It is a risk, a very high risk indeed that we will fail; Shingas may succeed and Robbie will remain dead, his life's energy returned to the universe. Thus, he will be gone forever."

Emily looked directly at me, not giving voice to the question I knew she wanted to ask. I replied "Yes, I understand the risks involved and I accept them of my own free will. I absolve you here and now, such that, if we should fail in our endeavor, and I do not return, it was not your fault. You are forgiven."

Emily turned to Ezerial. "How, exactly do you plan to provide a controlled death and then bring him back?"

"I was hoping to rely on your expertise with that phase."

Emily stretched her neck as if to prepare for a lecture. She grabbed the arms of the chair and scooted a little further forward. Assuming a matter-of-fact expression she began, "If we stopped his heart with a jolt of electricity from, say, a defibrillator; we could induce death without damage to the rest of his body. Unfortunately, his body itself would begin to quickly die if we don't provide oxygen to the brain and other organs. He might have a minute or two, far too short a time to deal with Shingas on any plane. He may return to his corporeal self, but what would be left would be a bag of rotting meat."

"What if you had every medical instrument at your disposal," Ezerial asked. "Could you sustain his body for say an hour or two?"

Emily sat there a moment, turning over the concept in her mind. After what appeared to be an eternity of deep contemplation, she replied, "It could be done, but we would need an enormous amount of technology, a sterile environment, controlled systems and medicines at the ready to manage any issues that may come up. We will need security, a private space to work. I can't have anyone in the medical profession know I am about to kill another human being, even if it is to save the world. We will need weeks to prepare; but I still don't see how it would work."

"First, I can assure you that everything you need will be at the ready. You will have direct access and control of the latest in medical instrumentation. We will have complete privacy. No one will know what we are doing, now or ever."

Emily looked surprised but held her tongue. Ezerial continued, "As for timing we do not have weeks or even days. There will be a full moon tomorrow night."

"What does the moon have to do with this?" interjected Dave, again showing his skepticism for the entire ordeal.

The moon is a powerful entity to the Native American Indian. It represents the female divinity, the yin if you will. To his tribe, the moon was the goddess, the feminine face of God. The moon is known to the Lenni Lenape as Grandmother Moon and is responsible for life, birth itself, if you will. Shingas will use the power of the full moon, absorb its energy and essentially be brought forth, as if in birth. The power of the moon cannot be underestimated. He will have one chance, and one chance alone. If he fails to come though, his power will be dissipated, and he will be lost to the universe forever. We must use this time to our advantage and obstruct his proverbial birth and end him forever. So, no, we do not have weeks, we have less than twenty-four hours to prepare and succeed."

While Ezerial was talking, Dave just sat there shaking his head and smiling. "This just gets better and better and better."

Paul finally stirred and asked, "I'm a little confused. You need Dr. Howell as a physician to medically induce death in Dr. Mauro and hopefully revive him some hours later."

"Yes," replied Ezerial.

"And you said you need Dave for his strength and conviction."

"Yes."

"You haven't mentioned me. Why am I here? "

"You, sir, play the most critical role in this quest," replied Ezerial, looking Paul straight in the eye. "For every great endeavor, for every important event in history or religion, there was a witness. One who stood within the inner circle as events transpired. A witness, who saw the event unfold, from beginning to end. It is the witness who decides the story itself, how it will be portrayed to the world, now, and in the future. The burden will be on you, Paul Mercuri, to determine what will be revealed and what will remain hidden. If we are successful and Shingas is destroyed, it will be your responsibility to report to your superiors, and perhaps, the public at large, what happened and how it was done, for they will want, and need, closure to this murderous rampage. If, on the other hand, we fail, and all is lost it will fall upon your broad shoulders, to tell the tale of our failure, and prepare the same superiors for what will happen next. I am afraid our jobs pale against your responsibility for you will choose what is revealed and what remains hidden."

Standing, Ezerial addressed the assemblage, "The hour of dawn approaches. We have precious little time and much to do. Are we all still in agreement that we are committed, of our own free will, to continue the journey and see it to the end, no matter what the cost?"

Almost in a single voice they replied, "Yes."

"Then let us go now and prepare ourselves. Clear your minds of interference for you will need all your intellect and all your energy to survive this journey. Pray, if you are so inclined, as I will pray to the almighty both for strength and forgiveness. Robbie, you, most of all must prepare. I cannot guarantee you safe passage. In fact, I believe the odds are against us, but it is you, and you alone, who can stop the horrors to come." Turning toward Dave and Paul, Ezerial continued, "Detectives, prepare your minds and bodies for the struggle we will face." Turning toward Dr. Howell I saw Ezerial's face soften as he addressed her. "Emily, my dear Emily, I truly understand the conflict within your heart and soul. You have sworn an oath to save and protect. I am asking you to forswear that oath and kill a fellow human being, all in the name of something you cannot be expected to understand. But understand this, you are forgiven now and forever, for the task that I have placed upon you is my burden to carry and not yours. I absolve you of this sin and offer to you the peace and love of God." With this he blessed us by making the sign of the cross. "In nomine Patris, et Filii, et Spiritus Sancti. Amen."

The trio repeated "Amen" as they each followed suit by making the sign of the cross with Ezerial.

"Go now and return tomorrow night at midnight. We shall reconvene, not here, but at a place I have prepared for the final phase of our quest. I have prepared a special private suite, at a location that is private and secure. Meet me this night at the corner of Somerset and Plum Streets, downtown New Brunswick."

Dave jumped in, "Isn't that the address for the Robert Wood Johnson Memorial Hospital? We are meeting in a public place?"

"I have prepared the way, now go. I will tell you more, all that you need to know and no more" With that, he bowed his head in deference to us all and left the room.

Chapter 48

We had the room to ourselves. Ezerial left the room, effectively dismissing us, and leaving us to our individual thoughts. I started to make my way toward the door when Dave spoke up.

"I thought we were supposed to do this quietly, not at the most public hospital in New Brunswick. How the hell can we do this in secret, in a place that is constantly open to peoples coming and goings? I just don't get it."

Dave was right. The Robert Wood Johnson Memorial Hospital is a 900-bed medical institution in the middle of downtown New Brunswick. It sits across the street from the railroad station and is visited by hundreds and hundreds of people every day. The facility boasts having the most up to date medical technologies at their disposal, exactly what we would need for this mission. Dave may be concerned about the public nature of the hospital. I knew, however, something that no one else knew, Ezerial always has a plan.

"Look, guys, I have known Ezerial for a long time, I know that sometimes he is a bit strange, he has his ways for sure, but he also knows what he's doing." I said. "We need a place that has the latest equipment that medical science has to offer, right? "

"Of course, we do, but---" began Emily.

"Wait," I said, interrupting Emily. "We need the equipment the hospital offers, we agree on that."

"Okay," allowed Emily.

"Okay then, Ezerial has his ways. When I 'came back' it was there at this very same hospital, in a private suite, fully stocked with medical equipment and personnel that never questioned what was happening with me. It is as if they knew enough not to ask any questions. They treated my condition, without questions. I have no idea how he does it, but he does it well. Okay then, let's have some faith. Before this is over we may need faith more than anything else. So, are we still doing this? "

"I guess so," responded Dave.

Emily hesitated then replied, "I guess we are better off with the hospital at our disposal. Sure, I'm still in."

"Me, too," echoed Paul.

"Good then, let's get some rest, if anyone really can at this point. We will return, there, as we have been bidden."

"Wait a minute, what about you, Dr. Mauro? Are you really prepared to die, supposedly again? No one really asked your commitment in this quest. Is this what you really want to do? This could easily be a one-way trip for you," Emily asked, her emotions coming through loud and clear. She was worried.

I was taken aback. It was really the first time that anyone asked me what I was thinking about this situation. I did die once, on my twenty-fifth birthday and I was not ready at all to be dead then. Was I really ready to be dead now? I stood there silently for a moment thinking. I took in a deep sigh

220

and replied, "As I said before, it was Ezerial who brought me back from the time and space between life and death. I didn't really trust him at that time, but, now, I do. He needs me. I guess you all need me to do this. I may be the only one who can do this, and it must be done. If Ezerial is right, and we don't stop Shingas and allow the veil between the living and the dead to be torn, who knows what will happen. I can't take that chance, so yes I am committed." I added, "I have one question however."

"What?" asked Dave.

"Are you all as committed as you need be?" The trio flashed a shocked visage across their collective faces. I continued, "Dr. Howell, you are about to potentially end my life. There's hope I may come back, but you will be causing my death. Are you really, truly, prepared?"

"I, like you, Dr. Mauro, see no other way. If you are as convinced as you seem to be to help Ezerial, then I, too, am committed to see this to the end. So yes, Robbie, I will kill you and do everything in my power to move heaven and earth to bring you back," responded Emily.

"Thank you for that. What about you, Dave? Are you really into this? You seem to be challenging what we are about to do. You may play a role as important as Dr. Howell. Ezerial said you supply strength. I have no idea what that means, but Ezerial said you are critical to what we are going to attempt, so I ask again, are you fully committed? "

Dave looked me in the eye and replied without hesitation, "Dr. Mauro, I am convinced from what I have heard that

221

there is nothing outside of this plan, crazy as it may be, that can stop this Shingas. I have no idea what I am supposed to do, but I can assure you that whatever it is I will give it my all. I want this over. So, yes, I am committed."

"Paul, what about you? You seem to have the easiest job?"

"I'm not so sure how easy my job will actually be," replied Paul a little uneasy. "Ezerial said that for every great event, there has been a witness. That witness will have seen all, but he and he alone will decide what is revealed and what is to be kept hidden. I will be witness to a death and resurrection, if successful. That is something to sing about, yet, I am sure that truth can never be told. I will also be a witness to closing the veil between life and death. Millions have searched for the truth of life after death or what is behind the veil. I will bear witness to these things, yet, I am sure this, too, can never be revealed. So, I will be forever in a crisis knowing what I know and not being allowed to tell the truth."

"Paul, are you okay?' asked Emily, sympathetically.

Paul was giving his reply deep consideration before he answered, "If what I know now, and what I will soon witness, will help solve this puzzle and stop something worse from happening, then yes, I too am committed to following through."

Somehow, I felt at peace within. I have no idea why, but I felt as if this is what I was meant to do, why I survived this long. I turned to the group and said, "Then, let us go and be alone with our thoughts. Let us prepare our hearts and minds to the task ahead. We have a few hours until we meet again. I bid you good day." I embraced them individually, holding them a moment, as if they were family, before I headed down the steps and back to Seaman street.

Chapter 49

The sun was fully up by the time I returned home. I looked at the sun behind the roof line and wondered if it was my last sunrise. I shook visibly, as if to shake off something clinging to my body, then headed up the porch steps and into the house.

As always, the house was quiet. I lived alone, no family, no pets, only a few plants to keep me company. For the first time in a long time I felt truly alone.

Suddenly, I was hungry. Not just hungry, famished! I needed to eat, and I needed to eat now! I headed down the hall and into the kitchen to fix something. I looked at the fridge, stocked with foods of every variety. As an Italian, I loved to cook, and so I was always making something special in honor of my mother or grandmother, both of whom were wonderful cooks. This morning I decided to go all out.

I fixed myself an omelet, loaded with Italian sweet sausage, green and red peppers, onions and, of course, pecorino Romano cheese. Next, I warmed some fresh Italian bread and slathered each slice with butter and strawberry preserves. I topped off my meal with a cup of dark coffee with a hint of hazelnut finish. I felt better, much better.

Since I was up all night with Ezerial and the others, I thought of going to sleep or at least try to get some rest. No way. I was too nervous. Excited? Scared? Either way sleep was not in the cards.

I got up from the table and headed to the sink where I washed, dried and neatly put away the breakfast dishes. Next, I cleaned the frypan, coffee pot and even wiped down the stove and counters. I know I was burning off nervous energy, but it made me feel good, centered in a way. This was just a normal day.

Suddenly it hit me; and hit me hard. This was not a normal day! I was going to die tonight. I was going to die, and somehow, I was supposed to stop some evil spirit from crossing through the veil between life and death. How I was supposed to do that? I had no idea. My body began to shake uncontrollably. I started to sweat, and my heart was pounding a rhythm that was close to a rock concert drummer. If I didn't sit down, and soon, I knew I would pass out.

I headed to the living room and fell into the couch's soft cushions. I calmed down a bit, but I was still shaking, and my mind would just not stop.

So, I am going to die, stop some mad spirit, and then, somehow, I was going to be revived and returned to this life? The concept kept rolling over and over in my head. The voice in my head would not silent. It screamed within my very soul. The whole idea was absurd. The worst part, however, was I agreed to the whole plan. I had to be out of my mind! I started to hyperventilate. I was getting pains in my chest. I started sweating profusely. I was having a profound panic attack. I stood there sweating and holding on to arms of the couch for dear life. I was going to faint or throw up or both. I was distraught.

Suddenly, as if out of nowhere, I heard the voice of Ezerial. I turned around looking for him; but of course, no one was there. The voice was in my head. At first, I thought it was my imagination, then I started to listen as I heard him say, "Robbie, all will be well. You are not alone in this. I am, and always will be, with you. Have faith. This is indeed a dangerous enterprise, one that may unfortunately fail. But you will not be alone. I will help guide you through. Have faith, and all will be as it should be. Success or failure, it will be as it should be."

I felt a little better. My heart slowly returned to normal, my chest pains subsided, and I could feel my entire body relax a bit. I inhaled deeply and exhaled slowly a few times to center myself. I said to the empty room, "Thank you. I do understand. I am not alone."

Feeling better I decided to head out for a walk, hoping to pass the time and to keep myself centered, calm and prepared for the events to come. I knew this could be my last day and I wanted to make the best of it.

I headed out the front door and just stood on my porch, a place where I loved to sit and read on warm summer nights. I remembered the nights I spent swinging on the porch swing reading and just enjoying being alive. I took it all in as if for the last time and headed down the steps and toward the University and my lab in the basement of Thompson Hall. I felt most at ease there; in control. I needed some control over events. In the next few hours all control over my life would be taken away, so I needed to be back at the lab, for one last time at least.

I walked along Nichol Street observing every little thing around me. A gray squirrel, hunting nuts, crossed my path and ran up a tree as I approached. He chattered at me from his perch on the tree, as if complaining that I ruined his hunt for nuts. I smiled and pressed on. As I moved closer to Thompson hall I noticed that the birds were singing in the trees. Upon closer inspection, I was able to see that they were blue jays. Noisy birds for sure. Today they were arguing back and forth as three or four birds could be seen jumping from branch to branch, each trying to drive the others away from some food source or some favorite perch. I could see that life was all around me. The animals, the flowers, even the very air seemed alive. I continued my walk and turned the corner onto Lipman Drive and followed the road to Thompson Hall.

Arriving at the side entrance to the basement, I opened the door and immediately was hit by the aroma of a science lab. There were the telltale smells associated with a bio lab, some faint odor of antiseptic mixed with acrid odors emanating from the animal cages we kept for experimentation. To some it was repugnant, but to me it was calming. I spent many years here in my first life and then decades in this life. It was home to me, a place where I belonged. I walked down the dark, ancient hall, and thought of all the people since 1921 who studied in these hallowed environs.

There was Selman Waksman and his research associate Albert Schatz, who co- discovered Streptomycin; Robert Cooke who discovered antihistamines; George H. Cook for whom the College was named, and on and on. I was in the presence of greatness when I entered these halls.

I walked down the hall, followed by the ghosts of those passed, and entered my lab. Standing at the entrance, I looked around. It was nothing great, just an old room, white tile walls now yellowed with age. Soapstone lab benches, cracked and marred by thousands of students who learned their craft where I now worked. In deference to those long gone, I straightened out the shelves, and put away the glassware I left out the last time I was here. I felt the need for order. I felt that if everything was in order here in the lab, it would also be in order with my life. I was tied to this lab and so it was a reflection of myself. It was as much a part of me as I was a part of it. I wiped down the lab benches and swept the floor. By the time I left, the room was in perfect order, ready for my return, or my replacement.

Leaving the lab, I headed out across the street to Passion Puddle, the large open area bordered by trees and often used by students and faculty alike for a rousing game of Frisbee or just sitting on the lawn, enjoying life to the fullest. As I got closer to the center of the parklike setting, I saw, off to my left, a tired old wooden bench under a huge old tree. That bench held special meaning for me. It was here that many years ago I met Cathy, a beautiful blind student, who once tried to help me cross over into the light. She was the last person I ever interacted with before meeting Ezerial and returning to this life. For old time sake, I sat on the bench and let my hands wander over the bruised and carved wooden slats, that over many years, bore witness to events untold. If this bench could talk, what wonders could it share?

It was growing late. I needed to get back home and prepare for the final ordeal that would begin this night. I needed to rest, fortify my heart and soul for the battle ahead. My journey was about to begin. I wondered, will this be my final journey? Only time will tell.

Chapter 50

I headed back to the house hoping to get some rest. I was physically exhausted, but my mind was racing a million miles a minute. I decided the best place to try at least to calm down was the attic loft. So once again, I tripped the secret lever, opened the hidden door and climbed the circular stairs to the loft.

Immediately, I felt calmer. I took a deep breath at the top of the stairs and let it out slowly, feeling at peace as I did so. I let my gaze roam around the room until I came to the Bentwood Rocker, with pillow and blanket, inviting me to sit. I accepted the invitation.

The rocker embraced me as I sat down. I covered my shoulders with the blanket. It felt as if it was a cloak of protection. I hugged my grandmother's pillow and promptly fell asleep.

It wasn't long before the dreams began. My father came first. He was as I remembered him, happy and full of life. He spoke to me saying, "Robbie, we are all so proud of you. You have done so much and yet there is more you must do. I know you are scared. I am, too, for you. We are all with you in spirit and should the need arise, you can call out to those who have loved you. We will be ready to answer the call." He reached out and touched my hand. I could physically feel his touch. He smiled and then he was gone.

I didn't have time to process what just happened for as soon as he was gone my mother came to me. She appeared dressed in her favorite dress. Her hair was made up as it was back in the 1900's, piled high on top of her head. She was, as I remembered, beautiful. Her smile was all I needed to know how much she loved me. "Robbie, my boy," she said, and then hugged me. I felt her arms around my body, even though I knew it was only a dream. I could breathe in her aroma; she smelled like a rose.

"Mom," was all I could muster.

"Shhhh, it's all right. I am here and will always be here. You are strong, stronger than anyone I have ever known. You are not alone." With this she kissed my forehead and was gone.

I was awash with emotion. Both my parents had the same message; I was not alone, yet alone I was. The contradiction was troubling. Finally, my grandmother came. She appeared as a middle-aged version of herself when she was at the height of her beauty. "Robbie, look at you all grown up! You are now a man, strong and powerful. The day ahead will be difficult and the task ahead dangerous, but you are not alone, we are with you always."

"Don't go!" I called, murmuring in my sleep. "I am afraid."

"Do not be afraid. You are surrounded by those who love you. Call out if you need us and we will always be there." And then she was gone.

I don't know how long I sat there in my grandmother's rocker, sleeping, but I do know I did not want to wake up. I felt safe here; I wanted to hold on to that forever. But it was not to be. Slowly, I woke from my reverie. I felt calm, at peace. My family was with me. I was not alone. I could almost feel them near. It was reassuring.

I stood up, slowly trying not to break the mood. Carefully, I folded the blanket and replaced the pillows exactly as they were on the rocker when I first arrived. I turned to head down the spiral stairs and to my fate when I heard a sound behind me. I turned to spy the rocker, slowly moving on its own, and knew I was not alone.

I was as ready as I would ever be. It was a little after ten p.m. when I returned to the main floor of the house. I decided to prepare a small meal to help me get through what was to come. I decided on a dish of fresh pasta, a few meatballs and a side of garlic toast.

My meal complete, the dishes done, there was nothing left to do. I headed out the front door and prepared to meet my fate.

Chapter 51

I headed down the porch steps and onto Seaman street. It was a short walk to Nichol Ave where I turned left and headed to George Street, the main drag to downtown. I was hoping to catch the last cross campus bus. The bus stop was in front of Voorhees Chapel at the corner of Nichol Ave. and George Street. I was surprised to find that I was the only person out and about on campus. Although it was not yet the start of the fall semester, I thought I would see someone on campus. I made my way over to the Douglass College student center. It was only eleven in the evening and surely someone would be out, I hoped, not wishing to be alone, but tonight I was the only soul about.

As I made my way to the bus stop, I did notice that it was unusually bright for this hour of the night. Unsure of why, I looked up into a clear sky as saw that the heavens were illuminated by an immense full moon. I was somewhat concerned at what I saw. I could see that the moon was not its usual white orb, but seemed to appear as if it glowed red. Then I remembered what Ezerial had said: Tonight was the blood moon, a time of great power for the spirit world. As the moon rose higher, it glowed brighter. There was no time to waste. I had to get moving, so I broke into a jog, and headed toward the bus stop.

Just as I crossed George Street, I could see the headlights of a campus bus approaching from the East. I stood alone at the bus stop; the driver applied the brakes, the squeal of which sounded as if a hundred demons were calling my name. I shuddered as the doors opened and stepped onto the empty bus.

"Good evening, Professor Mauro," came the greeting from the bus driver. "Beautiful evening."

I looked up to see Andy Wallace at the wheel. I knew Andy from the many times I traveled cross campus on the University transportation system. We had many interesting discussions. Andy was once a musician. He played guitar, wrote music and enjoyed the limelight for many years. He drove a bus in retirement for something to do. "Evening, Andy. Any new songs?" I asked just to make conversation.

"I'm working on a few. What brings you out tonight, Professor? It seems like only the dead are about," he chided.

"You have no idea," I said under my breath. "Just heading across town to the train station. I was hoping you could make an unscheduled stop close to the station. I am meeting some friends nearby."

"For you, Professor, sure. It's not like I'm going to put anyone else out!"

Andy shifted the bus into gear and we were off for the short mile and a half ride to my destination. Thankfully, Andy was not in a chatty mood, so we were both silent, lost in our own thoughts for the short duration of the ride.

Andy turned the bus onto French Street, in clear violation of the bus route protocol, and dropped me right in front of the train station. "Here you go, Professor. Have a drink on me." Andy opened the doors and let me off.

"Thanks, I will. Stay safe, Andy, and thanks again."

He smiled as he closed the door and put the bus in gear for the short ride to Easton and the end of the line at the bus garage. For a moment, I wished I was going with him, and not to my present destination. I watched as the bus drove off, hesitated a moment longer, then proceeded across Albany Street towards Little Albany Street. I walked down Little Albany and turned left on Somerset street right behind the main entrance to the Robert Wood Johnson Memorial Hospitals complex.

It seemed a bit odd to be walking down the backside of the hospital, away from the obvious main entrance, but Ezerial was quite specific. We were to meet at the intersection of Somerset and Plum streets. As instructed, I followed Somerset for three blocks and arrived at the precise location as set by Ezerial. I was not alone.

Standing there, at the corner, looking somewhat perplexed were my compatriots. I heard Dave ask, "Are you sure this is the right place? There is nothing here, no entrance except for this door and that appears to go nowhere."

Paul replied, "I'm sure he said here but, I dunno." Having spotted me, Paul called out, "Dr. Mauro, over here."

I waved acknowledgement and headed over to find, well nothing. We were at the back of the hospital with no obvious way of getting inside. There were entrances to the visitor parking garage, and, across Little Albany Street, an entrance to the employee garage. In front of where we stood, it appeared to be a door next to a tall white tank labeled "BOC gases." The door was painted gun metal gray and labeled with a sign that read "Do Not Enter. Authorized Personnel

235

Only. Property of RWJMH. There was no doorknob or any obvious way of gaining entry.

The three of us just stood there bewildered. Did we have the wrong location? How do we reach Ezerial? What do we do now?

Just then, the clock on the train station bell tolled midnight, the gray door, with its dire warnings, slid open and there stood Ezerial. "Good evening. Please, this way," he called, beckoning us toward the entrance way.

As it turned out, the door was not an actual entrance to the hospital but was a door to an elevator. Unusual to say the least to have a door from an elevator open directly onto the street. Also, peculiar, were the warnings on the door. Confused, I hesitated a moment before I stepped in along with Dave, Paul and Dr. Howell.

Ezerial reached out to press a button on the elevator control panel. I noticed something odd. There was only one button on the panel. There was not a choice of up or down, just one button, which Ezerial reached out and pressed.

The door slid shut with a hiss, as if we had just entered an airlock. There was no sense within the elevator to give any indication of movement. There was no jerk sensation indicating a direction up, nor was there the drop feeling, as if the elevator was falling into the bowels of the city. Instead, we stood there perfectly directionless for what seemed to be an eternity.

Quietly, the doors slid open, revealing a well-lit room of some kind. Ezerial exited first and, turning toward Dr. Howell, asked "Will this be sufficient?"

Chapter 52

Emily entered the room first. The look on her face was of pure astonishment. She stood in the center of the room, turning from side to side, and back again. Her face was a vision of pure incredulity as she surveyed the wide array of medical equipment before her. Amazed at what she saw, she stepped forward to get a closer look. Three of the walls were hospital white, shining as if just washed, while the fourth wall was a large window facing east. The window was shaded so that one could see out, but no one could see in. There was no idea what floor we were on, but it was high enough so that we had an unobstructed view over the city.

In the center of the room was a hospital bed with lighting and multi positioning remote control. On the left side of which, was an oxygen monitor and oxygen concentrator. Next to this was a pulse oximeter, with a ICU patient monitor and ventilator system. On the right side of the bed was a defibrillator, 3 channel EKG and EEG monitors. Next to this was another equipment station outfitted with a portable ultrasound scanner and a portable digital x-ray system. A CPAP / APAP system and endotracheal crash cart completed the station. On the other side of the room was a complete surgical suite, replete with operating table and operating theater quality lighting, anesthesia trolley, suction pump, and full set of sterile surgical instruments.

Adjacent to this was a mobile cardiopulmonary bypass unit. The system was designed to bypass the heart and lungs to allow for circulation and oxygenation of the blood to keep the patient alive. Today it will be used to keep the patient dead!

Finally, in the far corner, was a small lab set up, which included a blood chemistry automated analyzer, binocular scope hooked up to a flat screen monitor, hematology analyzer and mobile blood warmer system.

Emily turned to Ezerial and with a look of amazement said, "This will do. How did you put all this together? There must be a fortune in equipment in this room alone."

Dave and Paul just stood there, silent, impressed with all they saw, not truly understanding the half of what was in front of them.

"I wanted to make sure nothing was left to chance," Ezerial stated in a most somber voice. "If there's anything you may need, just ask and it will be provided. This room is secure. We will not be bothered."

"No, I think this is just about everything we may possibly need," replied Emily, still looking around and touching each piece of equipment. "This will be just fine," she repeated more to herself.

I felt a little more secure, just looking at all the equipment that can be brought to bear should it be necessary. I know Ezerial has no control over what was to come, but it was comforting to know he spared no resource to make sure that I had the best chance of coming back. I turned toward Ezerial and whispered, "Thank you."

He merely smiled and nodded.

I knew time was of the essence, so I said, "Shall we get this show on the road?" trying to exude more confidence than I really felt.

Dr. Howell broke her silence and said, "Yes, yes, of course. We need to prepare the patient," referring to me as if I was not in the room. I think she was trying to distance herself from what she was about to do, that is kill me. I sensed how difficult this must be for her. I felt sorry to put her through this, but it was the only way. Stepping up toward the bed, I asked, "What's the plan?"

Before anyone said a word, Ezerial stepped up and said, "Before we discuss what comes next, I would like us all to take a minute and join me in a prayer."

"Of course," came the reply in unison from the assemblage.

We formed a semicircle around Ezerial and, uncharacteristically, joined hands. We bowed our heads in reverence for Ezerial who began, "I call upon my brother, Michael, the Archangel, first of his kind. Glorious Prince, Chief and Champion of the heavenly hosts, Guardian of the souls of men, Conqueror of the rebel angels! Defend us in the battle to come. I ask that you use your mighty shield to protect us in our quest, wield, in your right hand, your sword of righteousness. Defend us against all evil that may come forth from the bowels of hell to defeat us. Michael, my brother and Prince of the heavenly host, we humbly pray for your intercession and with the host of angels at your command, help and protect us from harm. Amen"

We all repeated "Amen" while making the sign of the cross.

240

After a moment of silence, Emily began, "First I want to take the patient's vital signs, so we have a baseline from which to work. I will need blood samples, pulse ox, and blood pressure."

"Okay, then what? "I asked, hoping to ease her obvious pain.

"I will hook you up to the monitoring equipment, EEG and EKG so we can determine the point of, ah..." She couldn't say it, so I said it for her.

"Point of death."

"Yes, yes, the point of death." She was again visibly shaken but continued her lecture. "Next, I will administer some valium to bring the patient into a calm state and to act as an amnesiac, so you do not remember too much. I will use a high enough dose to cause the patient to lose consciousness. Once the patient is unconscious, I will insert a venous line in preparation for administration of any medications we may need during the death state and resuscitation process. While the valium takes effect, I will wrap him in a cooling blanket to drop his body temperature."

I thought that was unusual. "Why the cooling blanket?" I asked. As a biologist, it piqued my interest.

"If I lower the core temperature, the body will decay more slowly, giving us more time in the death state, before irreversible effects may set in. Also, once we resuscitate you, I can use the blanket on warming cycle to bring your core temperature up quickly, which should help in the resuscitation process.

"That makes sense, go on," I prodded

"How is the connection to the bypass accomplished?" I asked hoping surgery was not involved.

"Before we administer the shock to the heart and once you are completely sedated, I will insert a direct line cannula through the chest wall directly into the heart's right atrium. This will allow for controlled withdrawal of blood from the body. The blood will be mixed with an isotonic solution, similar to Heparin, to keep the blood from clotting. Blood will then pass through the machine which will allow me to oxygenate the blood, warm or cool the blood as may be necessary, then return the oxygenated blood to the body through a second cannula inserted into the femoral artery in your right leg. By continuing the circulation of blood throughout the body while the heart is stopped, we can prevent any long-term organ damage, which may occur from the lack of circulation. The pump will also aid me in the resuscitation process, allowing me the ability to warm the blood to normal, so the cardiopulmonary unit will serve a number of purposes." Emily hesitated then asked, "Any questions?"

Not having any, I shook my head no and she continued.

"Once I have the body temperature lowered to eighty-three degrees, I will add a bolus of Heparin to the IV line to prevent the blood from clotting once the heart has stopped. Finally, I will administer a shock to the heart using the defibrillator. This will interrupt the cardiac rhythm. I will then administer a shot of Lidocaine and Adenosine that will essentially freeze the heart in the resting state. Within seconds, the death state will be achieved. We can monitor your status using the EEG and EKG monitors." Emily breathed a sigh of relief as if just saying what she was going to do was difficult.

"Well, I agree, shall we?" I asked, beginning to doff my clothes, preparing myself to die.

Chapter 53

While I stripped down to my shorts, Dave and Emily laid out the cooling blanket on the bed. "Before we wrap you in the blanket, I need to put the EKG and EEG leads on you," stated Emily, as she prepared to move forward.

"Okay," I replied, a little nervously. I walked over to the bed, laid down, and Emily began by first fitting me with what appeared to be a hat made of fabric with a series of leads coming out of it.

As she fit me with the hat, she explained, "This is an EEG electrode cap that will allow me to monitor brain activity."

Once my "hat" was in place, she began to place a series of electrodes on my chest, sides and ankles. Again, she explained, "These electrodes will be connected to the EKG monitor, which will monitor heartbeat and electric impulses in your body. This will help in the resuscitation process and will confirm the death state." Once I was "connected," Emily asked, "Robbie, are you comfortable?"

"Yes, thank you." My voice cracked, confirming my fear.

Emily put a hand on my shoulder providing some support to belay my fears. She smiled at me, nodded, and then turned to Dave and Paul. "Guys, if you would, please carefully wrap Robbie in the blanket, leaving his arms and lower legs free. I will prepare the IV lines."

Dave and Paul stepped forward and, silently, began, very carefully, as if I were made of glass, wrap the cooling blanket over my chest and legs, being very careful not to disturb any of the leads. Paul hands were visibly shaking. Dave, however, was more stalwart, as if he knew and accepted this was our only option. Once I was comfortably wrapped in the bed, they stepped away and Emily stepped in.

"Robbie, I am going to insert an IV line into your right arm. This will be the main line. I will also insert a secondary line into your left arm just in case. Is that okay?" she asked as if I were a patient and I had a choice. "Once the line is in, I will administer a dose of Valium to help you calm down. Once you are calm, I will increase the Valium load. In a few minutes, you will lose consciousness and from then on you will feel nothing."

"Okay," was all I could muster. This was really going to happen, I thought. I am about to die. My heart rate visibly jumped on the monitor.

Emily inserted the IV line with such efficiency that I didn't feel a thing. She administered a minimum dose of Valium, designed to calm me down and return my heart rate to a normal rhythm. When she was done, she shot me a nervous smile and patted my hand. I smiled in return. We were both scared to death.

Emily then ran an EEG and EKG strip as a baseline. She checked all the monitors, confirmed the placement of all the leads, checked the IV lines again. She seemed to be looking for anything to do, except move forward. Soon, there was no longer any cause for delay. It was time for the final procedure.

Taking a deep breath, she let it out slowly. Wiping the hair from her eyes, she looked around the room at those present and asked "Ready?"

Everyone silently nodded.

"Okay then." Turning toward me, she said, "Robbie, now I will increase the level of Valium until you lose consciousness. Once sedated, the next step will be to administer a cardiac shock to stop your heart. Once it is stopped, I will administer the Lidocaine/Adenosine cocktail through the IV line to bring the heart into stasis."

At this moment Ezerial stepped forward and came over to the bed. "Robbie, once you are released you will need to go to the Raritan River Conservancy. There you will find Shingas. He has a brief window within which to cross the veil. As you may recall, the energy of the living is at its lowest at three a.m. The spiritual energy is consequently at its highest. At that hour, the blood moon will be at its zenith, and thus the spiritual energy will favor Shingas. He will have to transition before sun up, so there is a three-hour window for him to cross or for you to stop him."

I nodded but added, "How do I stop him?"

"By any means necessary," was his reply.

"I understand," I said, but not sure if I really did.

"Remember, you are not alone, I will always be with you. Call upon the powers around you for strength. You are not alone." He made the sign of the cross on my forehead and stepped back. Turning toward Emily, he nodded, giving his consent to proceed.

Emily looked over at me as she inserted the valium dose into the IV line in my arm. She kept smiling at me, even though I knew she was terrified as was I. As the dose traveled through the line and entered my body, I began first to feel lightheaded. I tried as hard as I could to keep my eyes open, fighting to the last to remain conscious, but to no avail. I could no longer delay the inevitable, I fell into unconsciousness.

Emily, once again, took a deep breath and let it out slowly. She turned toward Dave and Paul and asked, "Ready?" They nodded. She stepped forward with the defibrillator paddles in her hands. She spread the electroconductive gel on the paddles, then worked the paddles together spreading the gel. She reached out and touched a button on the defibrillator paddle and called out, "Charging to 260." The unit responded by emitting a high-pitched whirring sound which changed in pitch as soon as the paddles were fully charged. Without further preamble, she called "Clear," and hit me with an electric shock.

Chapter 54

The jolt was so intense that my body jumped off the bed and nearly onto the floor. Every muscle in my body contracted, my back arched, my legs stiffened. My entire body lifted off the bed in one huge convulsion, then, suddenly, it was over, and I was looking down at myself!

I could see me lying in the bed. Emily had a look of horror on her face as she watched the EKG monitor go flatline. Dave and Paul just stood there, first looking at me, then at each other and then back to me. They had just killed another human being, and their expressions were horrified. What they had just done conflicted with everything they believed in and fought for. They were murderers in their own mind. The room was dead silent save for the EKG alarm, which shrieked, indicating cessation of life. I was dead.

Emily finally mobilized and reached over to silence the alarm. I heard her say, "I will now administer the Lidocaine/Adenosine shot into the IV." She reached out to administer the shot, her hand was shaking so much she withdrew, looked down to calm herself before she tried again. This time she was successful.

Reaching over to the cardiopulmonary unit, she switched it on. Blood immediately filled the line coming out of my body as the pump drew a low-level vacuum forcing the blood, my blood, toward the machine. Within a few beats, blood appeared in the second tube and made the short journey from the pump system, through the second line, and into my femoral artery, back into my body. The circuit was complete.

248

My heart was stopped, my brain was flatlined, but my organs were alive, perfused with oxygen enriched blood.

Ezerial then stepped forward and addressed Dave in somewhat of a commanding voice. "Dave, Robbie needs your strength if he is to survive this night."

"What can I do?" asked Dave confused.

"Put your hands on his shoulders and keep them there. Your life's energy is strong, stronger than I have ever seen. Your strength, your energy can be used to pass into Robbie, giving him strength here in this room and out there where his is preparing to do battle. Hold him and allow your power to flow from you into him. His success and his very life depends on you."

Dave immediately acted. He stepped forward, rubbed his hands together as if to warm them, and touched my body in the bed.

As he made contact, I could immediately feel the energy within my current state change. I felt stronger, more powerful. I knew Ezerial was right. I was not alone. I looked around at the scene before me. Paul stepped forward, unbidden, and put his hands on my ankles. Ezerial gave him a quizzical look. Paul said, "It can't hurt, right?"

"No, it can't. Thank you," offered Ezerial with a smile.

Suddenly, there was a voice, a voice out of nowhere directed at me. "Robbie, there is no time to waste. It is nearly two a.m. You have been released from this body, go; go now. Seek

249

Shingas before he crosses the veil. Go. Stop him or all is lost. You are not alone." The voice was that of Ezerial. His body was looking at mine in the bed, but his mind was with me.

I replied, "Yes, I understand."

The dead are not limited in transport as are the living. We can move about freely, through solid objects and over great distances in the blink of an eye. I hesitated a moment, looking down at myself, then I was gone.

I was suddenly outside. My energy had traveled to the conservancy at a bend in the river very close to the spot where the body of the Colonel was found. I was drawn to this spot by something; I soon found out what.

Looking around, I noticed the night was not dark. Even though there were no lights shining from civilization, the night was unusually bright. I was amazed to see the moon, the blood moon, sitting high in the sky radiating a cool light over the area giving an eerie glowing look to the surroundings.

The moon itself looked red, as it reflected the light from the sun on the other side of the horizon. It cast a sinister glow to the surroundings. I could feel the energy around me. All was quiet. I was concerned, for I had no idea where to find Shingas, let alone stop him. As I contemplated what to do next, I heard a sound. It was a sound that scared the hell out of me.

I heard a chanting, almost as if the sound came from nowhere and everywhere at the same time. I tried to localize the source and headed closer to the water to get a better feel.

There, under the light of the moon, was a shimmering figure. It was Shingas. He was on his knees, arms raised high above his head, in the direction of the moon. He was chanting. I moved closer to get a better lock on what he was saying.

"Hey-a-a-hay! Lean to hear my feeble voice. At the center of the sacred hoop, Grandmother moon hear my voice.
You have said that I should make the tree to bloom.
With tears running O Great Spirit, my Grandmother, with running eyes, I must say....
The tree has never bloomed.
Here I stand, and the tree is withered.
Again, I recall the great vision you gave me.
It may be that some little root of the sacred tree still lives....
Nourish it then, that it may return to life and bloom so that it may fulfill your prophecy!
Hear me, Grandmother, that I may return to seek my vengeance against those who have destroyed your people."

I was shocked. Here was Shingas, his spirit at least, praying to the moon to grant him passage through the veil. I moved closer to get a better view. He continued:

"Oh, Great Grandmother Moon Spirit, whose voice I hear in the wind, whose breath gives life to all the world.
Hear me; I need your strength and wisdom.
Let me walk in vengeance, let my eyes ever behold the red blood of mine enemies.
Make my body strong and my hands weapons; let my eyes see death in mine enemies, let my ears hear their wailing.

Make me vengeance, so that I may return to mine enemy that which
he gave to my people, Death.
Help me to remain strong in the face of all that comes towards me.
Grant me this prayer, Grandmother Moon, so that the name of
SHINGAS will reverberate throughout the land."

I had to do something to stop him, but what? I knew from
experience that the energy of the dead could be disruptive if
two dead entities' energies came close together. But was I
strong enough? I could physically feel the strength, the pure
energy, emanating from the spirit of Shingas, even from this
distance. *Am I strong enough?* I questioned with the voice in
my mind

I hesitated to move, hearing another voice in my head. "You
are not alone. I am with you. My strength is your strength.
Those who have loved you are with you. You are strong. Go,
go now and confront Shingas before it is too late." It was of
course the voice of Ezerial, he had become the voice in my
head. Guiding me, offering his strength. I felt a little better,
my doubt no longer held me cataleptic. It was time to act.

Chapter 55

"Time of death, one fifty-seven," announced Emily, as required by the medical code of ethics. "It's out of our hands now." Moving to the side of the bed, she turned a dial on the cooling blanket. "I want to take the body temperature down to sixty degrees. The record lowest temperature a person survived, was a drowning victim, who fell through the ice and had a body temperature of fifty-six point seven degrees. I don't want to go that low, but anything we can do to slow the decay process will give us a few extra minutes."

"So, what do we do now?" asked Dave, his hands still firmly affixed to my shoulders.

"Now, we wait," responded Ezerial. "Robbie will travel to where he can find Shingas. It is up to him to stop him. We can offer our good intentions and our strength, but he, and he alone, has to stop him."

"I don't understand," asked Paul. "How can Robbie do anything? He's dead. What can he do?"

Ezerial replied, "Life is measurable. So is death."

Paul said, "I don't get it."

"While we are alive we have energy, measurable energy throughout every cell and process within the body. Our brain is a series of electrochemical processes, all of which elicit measurable energy."

"Sure," Paul agreed.

"Our hearts beat because of electrical energy, which is controlled by the Sinoatrial node, "added Emily.

"Yes, correct. This energy is measurable. We even have names for it like Basal Metabolic Rate, which is the energy consumed when the body is at rest. The energy output is measurable, as we see here with the EEG, measuring electrical brain activity. The monitor is measuring the electrical energy of the heart and shows us that energy in a waveform called a QRS complex. The wave shows us the electrical profile of our heartbeat. All of these energy sources, when combined properly, keep us alive."

"Okay, I get that, but Robbie is not alive," Paul said.

"Yes, and we see that the energy of the brain has ceased, we call that flatlined. There is no measurable energy associated with his heart, as well. These conditions, no measurable brain or heart activity, constitute a medical definition of death."

"Okay."

"We have then to understand where this energy goes. In physics, the law of conservation of energy states that the total energy of an isolated system in a given frame of reference remains constant — it is said to be *conserved* over time. In other words, this law means that energy can neither be created nor destroyed; rather, it can only be transformed from one form to another. There is a world of understanding beyond this world. Created by the Creator long before time. This is the place of the nonphysical realm. You call it spiritual. Man is not designed to understand this realm, but it exists. That is where Robbie will do battle with Shingas. Their energy, the life form that they once had in this world, is now transported through death, to the next world. From time to time, under certain conditions, we see these worlds come closer and closer together. Tonight, because of the blood moon, and the energy accumulated by Shingas during his murderous rampage, these worlds have come very very close together; so close that a tear in the fabric that separates them can allow Shingas to pass. That is where Robbie is right now. He is near, yet he is far from us in time and space."

"Ok, I think I get it. Well not really, but after all I have seen and heard, I can accept it. But… how do we know? How do we know if he is successful and how do we get him back?"

"Paul, have faith," was all Ezerial said.

Paul was silenced. He remained at his position at the foot of the bed holding Robbie's feet, thinking, witnessing.

Chapter 56

Cautiously, I moved toward the clearing. I approached from behind, keeping low to the ground, hoping not to be seen. He was kneeling, with arms raised, chanting. I hung back for a moment. Shingas remained focused on the moon and the river flowing past. This was my chance. I moved forward and prepared for confrontation.

I could feel the energy of Shingas grow stronger as I approached. If I could feel him, could he feel me? It didn't take long to find out.

I was still more than twenty-five yards away when Shingas stopped chanting and rose from the ground. He turned full circle, seemingly sniffing the air as if to catch my scent. As he came to look in my direction, he stopped. I had been found, there was no turning back now.

With all the courage I could muster, I shouted, "Shingas, I call upon you to stop. I cannot, will not, allow you to cross the veil and gain access to the living plane. Your time has come and gone. There is no place for you, or your vengeance, among the living. I demand you stop now!"

He did not hesitate a moment. "I am Shingas, Great Medicine Man of the Lenape. Who dares to address me so? Come closer and kneel before me in supplication; for I will cross to the plane of the living and I shall have my vengeance." His voice sounded like thunder rolling over the river bank towards me. I could suddenly feel the power emanating from his spirit. I was outmatched and knew it; I think he knew it, too.

I hesitated not knowing what to do next when again Shingas spoke. "I am son of the Great Spirit, Kitanitowit; I am brother to the four winds. My power comes from Mother Earth; my spirit grows strong by the power of Grandmother Moon. I have become the Skadegamutc; the Ghost Witch. I will not be denied. Come stand before me and bear witness to my power!" I heard a rolling of thunder follow his words. Lightning flashed across the sky, attesting to the power Shingas wielded. Then the land fell silent; the only sound was the rushing waters of the Raritan River as they passed the spot where we stood.

I was terrified. I felt weak, unsure of my ability to succeed. Shingas was more powerful than I could have ever guessed. Standing before him, I could feel his energy radiating toward me, impacting my own energy, draining it. I grew weaker by the second. I had to do something, and quickly, before he drained what little energy I had left.

I rose from my spot and looked up toward the heavens and called upon those who have gone before me. In imitation of Shingas, I raised my hands high above my head, my eyes towards the heavens, and prayed. "I call to my mother, born of her flesh, having given me life, I pray, come to me now! I seek your strength, borne of love for your son. I call out to my father, he who planted the seed of life, he who raised me to be a man, come now, bring your power and strength. Stand by my side and aid me in my battle. I sing my call to my grandmother, she who loved me most of all. Come, bring your love and grant me the power to defeat mine enemy." For a moment I felt nothing. I began to lose faith. I began to feel alone. I was defeated.

Shingas heard my words and stood his ground. Suddenly, out of nowhere I felt a wind, not borne of the air, but carried by the spirit. I was struck back again and again as the wind hit me. Each time I felt my strength of spirit grow stronger. From out of nowhere, I heard and felt an energy respond. "We are with you," I heard the chorus call. I was no longer alone. My family had answered my prayer; yet was this was not enough? I felt stronger, yes, but Shingas was stronger still. I needed more. So once again I called out, "Ezerial, Firstborn of Creation, hear my prayer. Come, bring your strength and help me defeat our enemy."

I could hear Shingas sneer as he called out, "Go, call upon them all, for even together, you will not defeat me. I have nurtured my hatred for more than a century, building, growing stronger, until this night, when I will cross over to the plane of the living, where I will have my due. I shall become the living spirit of vengeance. Never seen but always felt. I will destroy mine enemies." Again, he raised his arms to the heavens and gave out a howl that shook the very ground upon which I stood. "Come let the battle begin!"

I could delay no longer, I moved closer. I felt his power pushing against me with every move forward. He was drawing my spirit energy, pulling it into himself, growing stronger as he drained me. I knew if I continued, it would be over before it began.

I stopped, realizing there was no way I could defeat him in battle. I needed another way. Suddenly, it came to me, something Ezerial said. Shingas has only one chance to cross over. He must do it this night, before sun up, or the veil will close and Shingas will have forever lost his chance to cross over. I couldn't defeat him, of this I was sure, but perhaps I could delay him long enough that the veil will close, and he will remain trapped.

I had a plan. I "died" at two a.m. Sunrise was a little after seven. I had no idea what time it was right now, nor did I know if time was measured in the same way for the dead as the living, but there was a chance. If I could find a way to engage Shingas, delay him somehow, distract him until sunrise, maybe, just maybe, the veil would close and Shingas will be defeated. I had no other options and decided to try.

"Why do you seek vengeance against men whom you do not know?" I demanded, hoping to engage him and deflect him from his quest.

He laughed. "I was the first and last of my kind. Born the son of a chief, I learned the healing powers, so I could help my people. We were a peaceful people. We were on this land since the beginning of time. We respected Nature. The buffalo was my brother. We killed only to survive, and when we did, we honored the fallen and gave them thanks for their sacrifice."

"So, you are a man of peace, of honor, why now do you seek vengeance?"

"As I grew, I learned how Nature and my people were one. We were part of the land and the land was a part of us. I used the gifts of Mother Nature to heal my people. We were at peace. Then the white man came. At first, we were afraid. We had not ever seen their kind. They were different, their clothes, their words, their customs; all were strange to us. We kept our distance. There was much land, land enough for all."

This was good. I had him distracted. Time was moving forward. I could see the night sky, ever so slowly, growing brighter. The sun had not yet begun to rise, but it wouldn't be long now. I needed to keep him talking. "Tell me, what happened?"

"This was our land, and we were willing to share but the White Man decided it was his. And so, he took the land, killed my brother the buffalo and cleared the forest. No matter how much land he took, it was not enough. He wanted more. And he continued to take, to steal and to kill my people and all the native people. They showed no mercy, their greed and hatred for our kind drove them, so we fought back."

I knew some American history, but it was always from the side of the Europeans. This was the first time I heard the story from the other side. I knew the white man had fought against the Indian, but, hearing the story from another point of view, gave me pause.

After a moment he continued. "The white man is truly stupid."

"How so?" I asked.

"If some Brave steals from another Brave, the thief expects that the offended Brave will try to get the property back, even to the point of killing the thief if it is merited."

"Okay," I replied, "I can see that."

"Not the White Man. When he decided the land was his, when he stole it from my people, did he not think we would fight to take it back? No, he did not; and that was his mistake. When I looked into his eyes before I killed him, I would only see surprise, surprise to learn that I was killing him to take back what he stole, what was rightfully mine. The White Man has no respect for the land. He wants it all, no matter who he takes it from. He took it all and yet still this was not enough."

I could hear despair in his voice, and I began to feel sympathetic to his plight. But I had to keep him talking, I had to keep him distracted. "You are right, Shingas. Our history with your people was not a righteous one. We did steal the land from your kind. We were brutal in our treatment of the Native Americans. We destroyed the great herds of buffalo that roamed the land. For this, I, too, am filled with regret, but that was long ago."

With a thunderous howl that shook the earth, Shingas roared, "Long ago? Your kind continues to take and take some more, and they give back nothing. Your kind has polluted the water, so it can no longer quench our thirst. Blackened the skies so that it no longer breathes fresh. The land you have turned to a place for refuse. Long ago?" he roared again. "I say not."

He was right. Our kind has raped Mother Nature. We have taken all she has offered and given back nothing. Our skies are polluted; our clean water scarce. The very land beneath our feet is strewn with the refuse of man.

"Again, I say you are right, we have not been good stewards of all we have." I was losing this argument." What we have done to the land and its native peoples should indeed condemn us." I hesitated a moment, then continued, "But, in this I can't allow you to succeed. Your time has come, and it is now gone. There are many among us, good righteous men and women, who fight for Mother Earth. On her behalf they rail against pollution, provide access to clean water and fight to stop further destruction. They must have the time, their time, to fight the good fight."

"Did your kind not kill my people? Did not your kind rise up against our women; our children, and butcher them as if they were vermin to be destroyed? Mine own son, a baby of two. I witnessed a soldier dash him against the rocks, splitting his head open before my very eyes, for the white man did not think his life was worth the price of a bullet. My own death, at the hands of soldiers, men of honor, was torture. They staked me to the ground, cut off my hands and feet so I could not enter the final hunting grounds. They left me there, staked to the ground, to die in agony. You ask me to spare these wretched excuses for men? No, I will not!" Again, his anger manifested in the eruption of thunder and lightning.

I was defeated. His arguments were sound. I had nothing else to say in our defense, so I said nothing, yet I knew I could not let him crossover.

"Stand aside, for the hour grows late. The dawn is coming, and I must cross now!"

I looked to the east and sure enough the sun's first rays had marched over the horizon. If only I could delay him for a few

262

more minutes. I had to prevent him from crossing the veil. If I could continue to distract him, his chances would be lost.

Shingas spoke again as the light rose and the thunder rolled, "Stand aside or I will destroy you here and now!"

I knew there was no way I was strong enough to defeat him. I could see and feel his power grow stronger as the anger within him drew more and more energy from the surroundings. I had no choice, however, but to try. If I lost this battle, I too would be forever lost, but I had to try.

I approached as if I was prepared to do battle. In a hopeless attempt to stop him, I pushed out all my energy at once, hoping to surprise him and catch him off guard. He responded by stepping forward and absorbing my feeble attempt to stop him. In my effort to weaken him, I unfortunately made him stronger.

I was weakened near to the point of extinction. I held on to the miniscule amount of energy I had left, refusing to be defeated so quickly. I dropped to my knees and raised my arms toward the heavens and called out, "Help me!" I didn't know what else to do.

Suddenly, there was a thunderous crack of light from the skies above. It was not lightning, for it did not flash and disappear. This light grew, stronger and brighter, as it traveled across the sky, illuminating the clouds. The light grew in intensity, until it coalesced to form a solid beam of incredible white light, which carried down to the ground and the very spot where I had fallen prostrate. The light began to form into a figure. I was terrified. I rose and turned toward

Shingas, who had taken a step back in amazement. I turned once again toward the light beam as it formed a more solid figure within.

Shingas took another step back, clearly frightened of this power I had called upon. He thought he had won the battle, as did I, but now things were changing. As the light grew brighter, the figure within fully formed. I could make out a person within the light, a man, it seemed, of great height. He was garbed in a white robe and held a sword in his right hand; a shield in his left. I was shocked at what happened next.

The figure remained within the light, hiding his features, yet fully formed. From within the beam came a most powerful voice, which proclaimed, "I am Michael, the Right Hand of God, Defender of the Almighty and Protector of all his creation."

I fell again to my knees, not knowing what else to do.

"I am Shingas, the first and last of my kind, stand aside or I will destroy you!" Shingas replied, building up his anger and directing it at the white light and the figure within.

"I will not let you cross the veil. Your time has come and gone. Those who have harmed you also defiled the laws of the Almighty. They have been punished and will remain forever tormented in the lake of hell fire. Those you seek to harm now are innocent of the crimes of their forbearers. They do not deserve your vengeance. They will be protected by the mighty hand of God. Go now. Return your energy of your own free will. Go now to your ancestors, to the gods of your people. Return so that balance may be restored."

Shingas replied, "I will never stand aside! I shall cross the veil and have my vengeance. I have no fear of your god for I am one with the gods of my ancestors. Grandmother Moon will grant my passage across the veil. Stand aside and let me pass. I couldn't believe what was happening. Shingas was challenging Michael, refusing to yield. I could almost make out the face of Michael as it changed from placid to anger in an instant.

"I command you to stand down and go to your ancestors in peace. I will not let you pass. I command, you in the name of the Almighty, once again be gone."

Shingas refused to yield. He turned toward the heavens and lifted his arms in prayer. He stood there praying to his gods. Then, without warning, Shingas rushed forward as if to attack. From out of nowhere, and everywhere, came the wailing scream of a battle cry, as Shingas threw all his energy directly at Michael.

Without hesitation Michael raised his sword high above his head and pointed it directly at Shingas. Thrusting it forward, he shouted, "Be gone!" and a bolt of pure energy, in the form of an intense white light, leapt from the point of his weapon, directly at the very core of Shingas. When the beam came in contact with the energy field that was Shingas, it exploded, rocking the ground and sending a shockwave through the air that shook the surroundings; and then it was gone. Shingas was gone, he had been defeated, his energy sent back to the universe whence it came.

"Thanks be the Lord," said Michael. Turning toward me, he reached out with his right hand. A beam of energy, much smaller than that which he had just unleashed on Shingas, came toward me. I felt its energy within my very being and I grew stronger. I was able to stand.

"Thank you," was all I could say.

I could make out what seemed like a smile across the face of this magnificent being. "Please give my best to my brother, Ezerial. Tell him he is well loved." With this, he rose and was gone.

I stayed there a moment, amazed at what I had just witnessed. There were no words I could use to describe how I felt as the course of events unfolded. Once again, I fell to my knees and said a prayer of thanks. The sun was fully up, and the veil had once again closed. There was nothing left for me here. It was time I returned, but where was I to go? Ezerial told me about how to die, but he neglected to tell me how to come back.

Chapter 57

"What the hell was that!" shouted Dave.

"What? What happened?" Emily turned from the lab table where she was preparing the medications needed to revive Robbie.

"I don't know. I was holding Robbie's shoulders as Ezerial told me. Suddenly, I felt a shock, then his body jumped as if he just received a massive electric shock. I felt it go up and down my arms. Then, just as the wave left me, I felt a significant drain on my energy, as if Robbie were draining me dry. I had to let go. I thought I would pass out."

"The battle has been enjoined," replied Ezerial before anyone else could speak.

"Whadda mean?" Paul asked.

Walking toward the bed and looking down at the body lying there, Ezerial continued, "Robbie is now with Shingas. The jolt you felt was Robbie calling for energy. He must not be strong enough to do battle on his own." Ezerial reached out and touched the body, directing his attention to Emily who was still at the lab station, saying, "Robbie can't do this alone, he needs more that he has. Come step forward, all of you, and add your strength to the battle."

Without a moment's hesitation, Dr. Howell dropped what she was doing and stepped forward, adding her delicate touch to the body. Dave and Paul joined her, as did Ezerial. They all held tight to Robbie. Ezerial said, "Now, concentrate your

267

mind and energy. Focus on your contact with Robbie. As you are with him here, so you are with him there. Give freely of your energy, for if he fails, there is no telling what will happen next.

"Now, let us concentrate. Let us pray that our combined energy, our hopes and love for this man will help him in this battle." Ezerial closed his eyes and began to pray. "Dear Lord, Father, hear the prayers of your humble son! Your beloved creation is in peril. We beseech you to send your warrior angel, Michael, your son and my brother, to join the battle to save your creation, for we alone are not strong enough to do battle with the evil standing before us. We are weak in the face of such anger. Lord, answer our prayer!"

A collective "Amen" followed by silence.

"What happens now?" asked Paul, his hands still firmly locked around Robbie's cold ankles.

"We wait," came the solemn reply at something just above a whisper.

Each stood in the room, lost in their own thoughts, praying, holding on to Robbie, offering their strength and comfort. Time stood still. They could feel the pull on their bodies, as their energy was drawn by some unseen force. Ezerial stood firm, hands directly over the heart, looking toward the ceiling, his lips moving in silent prayer. He looked worried.

After what seemed to be an eternity, Dave was the first to break the silence. "It's growing light outside; sun-up is coming. We don't have much time!" The sound of fear in his voice was almost palpable. "We have to do something!"

In unison, they all turned to Ezerial who simply said, "We are doing all we can. Have faith."

Again, silence filled the room as they continued to focus their energies toward the body lying on the bed. Ezerial continued to pray silently. The others began to follow his lead, as they too prayed their own silent prayers, pleading for help and an end to this horror. Minutes seemed like hours.

Suddenly, a massive jolt came from Robbie's body. It was as if lightning had struck Robbie, causing a major electric shock to pulse through him and into those present in the room. Everyone was thrown off balance, including Ezerial. Dave was thrown so hard he lost his balance and crashed into the wall at the head of the bed. Paul threw up his hands as he stumbled backward, trying not to fall. Emily just screamed, as she released her hold.

"What the hell just happened?" Dave called out, rubbing the back of his head where he hit the wall.

"The battle is over."

"What?" came the collective question.

Emily, Paul and Dave looked first at each other, then at Ezerial.

"What do you mean the battle is over, how do you know? What's happening?" Emily's voice was rising with each word, as she began to approach hysteria at not knowing what was going on. Dave and Paul exchanged glances, then all directed their attention once again toward Ezerial.

Ezerial was calm, his face serene. The sun was full above the horizon, sunrise fully embracing the new day. Ezerial looked out the window, "Our quest is all but complete. As I told Robbie, he was never alone in this battle. He had you with him here and in spirit. Our prayers were answered. Robbie has won and Shingas is no more."

Not knowing what to do next, Paul, Emily and Dave looked first at each other, then at Ezerial. Their faces were a mixture of exhaustion, fear and confusion.

Emily asked, "What do we do now?"

"Now we bring Robbie back!"

Chapter 58

I stood on the banks of the Raritan, facing east, letting the morning sun's rays wash over me as Father Sol brought forth the new day. I was now alone. Shingas was no more and Michael, beautiful yet powerful Michael was gone. The river flowed peacefully as the morning dew began to burn off.

Another day had begun. I realized at this moment that only a handful of people would ever know the truth of what happened here, this night. How close we had come to evil incarnate crossing over and wreaking havoc on the innocent. I knew I could never speak of this, but it would be forever burned into my memory. I began to wonder, should I even try go back to my body and resume my life?

I had lived my life once. It was cut far too short, but through an act of fate, I was given the chance to live again. My second life was full and rewarding. I had accomplished my goals and, though I was alone, I was happy. All I could ever have asked for was mine. I was content, complete. Did I really need more?

I stood there on the banks watching the river flow with endless energy, never stopping, always moving forward never back. Why should I go back? I had a decision to make. Do I choose to return to my body, or is this the time I release my energy to the cosmos?

I was at a turning point. I knew it would be easy for me to give up the ghost, so to speak. I would just release my energy and that would be the end. No more worry, no more concerns. I would be free and complete.

271

Returning to my body, now that was another thing entirely! I had no idea how to do that. How do I even begin? Was I supposed to go back to the hospital? Should I stay here and … what? I had no idea. It seemed that I was at a crossroads, not knowing which way to turn.

Lost within my own thoughts, I suddenly heard a familiar voice. "Robbie, your task is complete, it's time to return"

"Ezerial? Is that you?" I asked with the voice inside my head.

"Yes, your friends are waiting for you. They are worried. You are needed here. Follow the path set before you and return. You are not alone. We are all here. Follow the path and come home."

Suddenly, I felt a pulling, as if another energy field had suddenly formed and was forcing me into it. In a panic, I began to fight it, to pull away. Once again, I heard the voice of Ezerial, "Do not resist. Follow the path and it will bring you home."

I stopped resisting. I could feel the energy building all around me. Suddenly I was no longer at the Conservancy; I was back at the hospital, in the private room looking down at the scene before me, detached yet connected.

Chapter 59

"How do we bring him back?" Emily looked to Ezerial for direction.

Ezerial stood lost in thought, his eyes closed, facing the body on the bed. His lips moved in silence as if trying to communicate with the dead. No one moved. They had no idea as to what was happening or what to do next; they just stood there like children waiting for the teacher to give them instruction. Suddenly, he said, "Dr. Howell, now is the time to revive Robbie. He is back with us and needs you to bring him home."

Emily shook as if to shake off the cobwebs that bound her and then went into action. Looking directly at Ezerial, she said, "First we will begin by warming the blood using the bypass unit. Dave, turn the temperature dial to eighty-six degrees and hit the timer for eight minutes. We want to raise the temperature slowly to prevent any sudden shock to the body."

Dave moved to the bypass unit and without hesitation made the adjustments. While the blood was being warmed, Emily prepared for the next step. "I am going to insert an endotracheal tube into Robbie so that we can have an open airway. We will force air into his lungs during the resuscitation process." With this, Emily reached into the instrument tray and withdrew a laryngoscope and confidently inserted it into Robbie's throat. Identifying the vocal cords, Emily continued by inserting the endotracheal tube into the trachea, the main entrance into the lungs.

273

Removing the laryngoscope, she then attached the open end of the tube to the respirator.

"Dave, body temperature, please," she called as if speaking with a trained assistant.

"Eighty-three degrees and rising," came the reply.

"Good, call out when we stabilize at eighty-six."

While waiting for the body temperature to stabilize, Emily moved over to the crash cart and began opening boxes containing the prescribed medications to be used during the resuscitation process. As she opened each box of prefilled syringes, she called out the name of each medication. "Adrenaline, amiodarone, adenosine, atropine, calcium chloride, epinephrine, sodium bicarbonate..." The list went on and on.

As Emily laid each syringe on the tray, Paul said, "Do we really need all that?" his voice was high pitched, and more than a little fear broke through.

"I just want to be prepared. Paul, I am going to need your help. I can't do this alone. Come over here, stand next to this cart and familiarize yourself with the labels on each syringe. I have laid them out in alphabetical order."

Paul approached cautiously as if he were afraid of getting stuck with one of the sharp instruments.

Emily continued, "Here is the port in the IV line," holding the port in her hand and showing it to Paul. "When I tell you, I want you to pick up the specified syringe, insert the needle right here and push the plunger. Can you do that?" she spoke as if instructing a child.

"Yes," came the reply.

"Good. Dave, do we have a stable temperature?"

"Body temperature reads eighty-six degrees and holding."

"Okay, everyone, let's begin."

Ezerial stepped forward. He put his hands on the body and asked the others to join him. Each in turn placed their hands-on Robbie's body. Ezerial raised his eyes toward the ceiling and said, "Father, I am your humble servant. I beg you listen to me, Father, and answer my calling, for I am helpless and weak. Listen, Father, to my prayer; hear my cries for help. I call to you in times of trouble because you answer my prayers. I am your son, deserving of your love and forgiveness. Turn to me and have mercy on this my friend, Robbie Mauro, who has giving his all in your name. Have mercy on him; strengthen him and save him from the clutches of death. Amen"

A chorus of "Amen" followed.

Ezerial kissed the body on the forehead, stepping back while making the sign of the cross. He looked at Emily and said, "It is in your hands now. We are with you"

The trio each made their own sign of the cross and returned to their positions, Paul at the crash cart, Dave at the bypass unit and Emily directly at Robbie's side.

Emily began with a deep inhalation, let it out slowly and said, "Dave, turn up the body temperature to ninety degrees, put seven minutes on the timer. Paul administer a dose of Epinephrine and I will begin CPR." Reaching over to the ventilator, she turned it on and announced, "Beginning ventilation." The machine came to life and began to pump oxygen through the endotracheal tube and into the lifeless body on the bed. The only sound was the whoosh, whoosh of the ventilator as pulsed at five second intervals.

"We need to get the body temperature to ninety degrees, once we get there, I will disconnect the bypass and begin cardiac compressions. We need to get the heart started."

Dave called out "Body temperature ninety degrees and stable."

"Turn up the heating blanket to ninety-eight, switching off the bypass and beginning cardiac compression."

Dave stepped over to the bed and said, "I am trained in CPR, let me start the compressions. You are going to be busy with the resuscitation process."

Stepping away from the bed, giving way to Dave to begin compressions, Emily said, "Keep the compressions hard and steady. The ventilator will manage pulmonary function. You only need to keep the heart pumping."

"Got it," replied Dave, as he began compressions.

Turning toward Paul, she said, "Paul keep an eye on the EKG and EEG monitors. Both are flatlined now as expected. I need to know immediately of any change in activity, especially in the EKG, as we try to bring Robbie's heart online. Once we get that, I can only hope brain activity will soon follow."

"Roger that."

"Dave, we need to get the heart beating again on its own before we can resuscitate."

Dave asked, "Wait a minute, I thought that shocking the heart was the way to get it started, no?"

"Actually, no. Robbie's heart is flatlined. There is no electrical activity present at all. Unless we can stimulate the heart to beat on its own, no matter how erratically, using the defibrillator will have no effect. We need the heart to respond first on its own. What you are doing now is essentially waking up the heart."

She turned to Paul. "Administer the sodium bicarb and another shot of EPI. Dave, when I call out, stop the compressions. Everybody ready?"

Paul administered the medications, Emily counted to fifteen and ordered, "Stop compressions." Dave stopped and pulled his hands back, but stayed close, in case he needed to begin again.

Everyone looked toward the monitors. Nothing. "Damn, Dave back on compressions, Paul administer another hit of the atropine. Follow that by another shot of EPI."

As Paul prepared the shots, he looked at Robbie, and said, "Come on big guy. Everyone is here waiting for you. Wake up!" He administered the drugs and called out, "Go."

"Dave, stop the compressions," Emily ordered again. Everyone turned toward the monitors. This time there was a beat, weak but a beat.

"Another shot of Atropine. Come on Robbie, time to wake up."

"Shot in," called Paul.

The EKG went wild. The monitor was a flurry of lines flashing across the screen. "Okay, we have something. Looks like we have sinus tachycardia." Turning from the bed she said, "Let's hit him with the paddles."

She reached over to the defibrillator and grabbed the two paddles. She coated each with the conductive gel, then rubbed them together to make sure the entire surface was properly prepared to make the best contact possible with the body. Reaching over to the control panel, she adjusted the dials and called out, "Charging to 200." The machine came to life and began emitting a high-pitched whirring sound as the system charged. A few seconds later, this was followed by a single beep, indicating the system was fully charged and ready to administer a shock to the heart.

"Clear!" she said and placed the paddles, one directly over the heart and the second on Robbie's side, and hit the trigger. Robbie's body jumped in response to the shock.

Returning to the monitor, Emily saw that the tracing had not improved. "We are still out of whack, I am going to hit him again. Charging to 200. Clear!" Emily hit Robbie again. The result was the same, the body jumped, the rhythm stayed erratic. "Charging to 360, we are going to blast this boy back home! Paul one final shot of EPI with a side of sodium bicarb please." "Onboard."

"Okay, Robbie, now or never. Clear!" Emily hit Robbie for a third time. Robbie's body nearly jumped off the bed, the weight of the heating blanket keeping him from hitting the floor. All eyes were on the monitor. The tracing was mildly erratic, slowly the tracing began to show signs of a normal sinus rhythm. After a few more seconds, the erratic heartbeat fell into line. "Normal function, he's back!"

The euphoria was short lived. Although Robbie's heart was beating, his brain waves were still flatlined. The body was alive, but no one was in there.

"What do we do now?" asked Paul.

"Now it's up to Robbie. He is here with us," replied Ezerial.

Chapter 60

I was present in the room, but not yet in my body, as I observed the frenetic ballet from my perch high above the scene, as the trio tried to bring me back to life. It was heartwarming to see these three people, strangers really, working so hard to bring life back to the dead. Dr. Howell was the conductor while Dave and Paul, clearly out of their element and far beyond their comfort zone, followed her instructions to the best of their ability.

It gave me pause to think that these people, people whom I just met, were so dedicated in their endeavor to bring me back from the dead. I was humbled. I knew from this I was not alone, that I needed to return to my body; but how? I was here, my body was there, but there was no connection. How was I supposed to bridge this impossible gap between the living and the dead? I had no idea.

When I thought all was lost, I heard Emily shout "Clear!" as she applied the defibrillator paddles to my body. I not only saw my body jump in response, but I felt a powerful jolt of electricity against my own energy as the paddles delivered their shock. Somehow, I was connected to my body, but I was still outside of it. The activity continued unabated, when Emily called out a second time, "Clear!" and once again I felt and saw the results as my body jumped before my eyes and the pulling against my energy intensified.

I began to reason, that, as they were working on my body, my energy, my life's essence, was somehow still attached to the body before me. Maybe, just maybe, if they could bring my body back to life, my energy would be naturally drawn home

280

to it? Why else would I feel the drawing of my energy each time the body was shocked. I wanted to shout, "Do it again, I am almost there!" but I knew no one would hear me as the dead are often ignored.

Fortunately for me, Dr. Howell was not one to give up easily. She shouted more directions to Dave and Paul for more medication and once again charged up the defibrillator.

"Clear!" she shouted and applied the paddles for a third time.

This time I felt the jolt grab me and pull me toward the body as I saw myself, one final time, nearly fall off the bed. Suddenly, I was not looking down anymore, I was in total darkness. Now, I was more than a little scared. I went from watching the scene as if disconnected, to who knows where. I felt strange, as if I was no longer unfettered, but not yet connected to anything. I was, for the moment, lost.

Suddenly, I felt warm, dizzy and my chest hurt like hell! I tried to inhale but my throat was blocked with something. I tried to move, but I didn't have the strength. Had I come back only to die in the bed?

"He's choking," Emily called as she reached over my body and began to pull out the endotracheal tube that was obstructing my airway. I felt every inch of the tubing as she pulled it out. When the last inch was removed, I sucked in a lungful of air and immediately began choking and coughing.

"Easy there, big fella, easy," soothed Emily, as she put her hand on my chest to help me calm down. "Welcome home!"

Dave reached over to Paul from across the bed and gave him a high five. Emily just looked down at me and smiled. She looked at the monitors, pulled out a stethoscope and checked my heart and lungs. She felt my feet to assess circulation and pronounced, "He's alive!"

Dave and Paul came around to the side of the bed and stood next to Emily. Dave gave her a hug congratulating her on her success at the impossible while Paul looked down at me and asked, "What happened?"

I thought for a moment and lied, "I don't know. I really have no memory of anything past the point when I died. I have no idea what happened."

Emily said, "That makes sense actually."

"How so?" asked Paul.

"I had hit him with a pretty heavy dose of amnesiac to ease him through the ordeal. Combine that with the fact that when Robbie was out of his body, in the energy state, he was not connected to his brain. Without that connection, his brain he could not make any memory connections, so he would not have access to anything that happened when he was not in his body."

Paul replied, "Makes sense."

Quietly, out of the shadows, came Ezerial. Looking across the bed at Dave, Paul and Emily he asked, "May I have a moment alone with Robbie?"

"Of course," came the reply as the trio left my bedside to busy themselves elsewhere.

Before Ezerial could say a word, I whispered, "I remember everything!"

"Of course," he replied. "What you have witnessed is far beyond the comprehension of man. You have seen the spiritual plane and survived to return to this mortal plane. What you saw, what you heard, must be kept within."

"I understand," I replied. Ezerial smiled. I smiled back and whispered, "I have a message from your brother, Michael."

"Oh?" he said, lifting his eyebrows ala Mr. Spock.

"He asked me to tell you that you are well loved."

This brought another smile to his countenance and he said humbly, "Thank you."

"What happens now?" I asked

"Now? Well, now you go on with the rest of your life, of course. There is much ahead for you, much yet to accomplish. Many stories to write and many days to enjoy. You are a most extraordinary individual, living a most extraordinary life. Make the most of it, but most of all, know that you are never alone. There are those who love you whether they are seen or unseen. They are with you always." He took my hand and gave it a squeeze. He followed this with a blessing and finished by making the sign of the cross over my forehead and heart, saying, "You are never alone."

Ezerial then looked up, caught Emily's eye, and said, "Dr. Howell, you are a most extraordinary person. Without you, and the help of your colleagues, none of this would have been successful. I thank you for your dedication."

Emily blushed and replied, demurely, "Thank you." She, Dave, and Paul approached the bed and began peppering me with questions, questions which I deflected by feigning lack of memory.

Ezerial laughed and said," Perhaps our friend needs a little rest after his ordeal. Please feel free to stay here as long as necessary, the facilities are at your disposal." With this parting comment, he opened the door to the elevator, stepped inside and was gone.

"Ezerial wait!" Emily shouted, but it was too late. The doors had closed. Turning toward me, she had a quizzical look. I knew she wanted to ask if we would see Ezerial again.

I answered her unasked question. "He does that, you know, disappears just like that. I know he is with us. We four now have a special bond with him. We may not see him again, or perhaps we will, who knows. I do know that he will always be with us. He is that voice in our heads, the one that whispers to us when we need it most. Ezerial is a Watcher, he is always Watching."

Epilogue

For the last three weeks Paul and Dave wrestled with what to put in their final police report concerning the murder case. The good news was that no more murders were committed since the night of Robbie's ordeal. Of course, the culprit was no more, but what could they possibly put in their report to close the case and still make it believable?

"Dave, we have come up with fifty different scenarios to close this case, and none of them makes any sense," lamented Paul as he finished another beer and reached for his third from the fridge in the war room.

"I know, I know," replied Dave, exhaling in frustration. "We have to come up with something. Captain will have our heads, if not our badges, if we don't close this case and soon."

"I suppose we could try some version of the truth?"

"Really? Let me see, Captain, the murders were committed by an Indian Spirit named Shingas who died about 250 years ago. We killed our friend, Dr. Robbie Mauro, so he could prevent Shingas from crossing the plane of the dead and entering the plane of the living.

Dr. Mauro was able to stop Shingas, so our colleague Dr. Emily Howell from the coroner's office brought Dr. Mauro back to life. Does that about sum it up?" offered Dave not attempting to hold back any sarcasm.

"Geeze!" Paul sat back in the chair and rubbed the top of his head when the phone suddenly came to life. "That's just what we need," Paul said, reaching for it.

"Detective Mercuri," Paul spoke into the mouthpiece. This was followed by a series of "yes, sir" and "no, sir." He then hung up.

"Who the hell was that?" demanded Dave as soon as Paul hung up the phone.

"Captain Capella. He wants us in his office now."

"Great! Nice way to end a career," Dave said bitterly, as he rose from his chair and proceeded up the stairs to what he expected was his doom.

"Can't be that bad," Paul offered.

Dave stopped on the third step, gave Paul a look and said, "Really! That all you got? Geeze!" Shaking his head, Dave continued up the stairs. When he got to the top he shouted to Paul, who was yet to move, "You coming?"

"Reluctantly," replied Paul at just above a whisper so Dave would not hear him, and he ascended the stairs to their fate.

They drove in silence to the precinct, each lost in their own thoughts as to what to tell the Captain. When they arrived, the duty sergeant stopped them from going to their desks by saying, "He's waiting for you in his office."

Looking a little aghast, Dave said, "Does everyone know we were called to the principal's office?"

The duty sergeant replied, "Yup," as he pointed again to the Captain's office.

"Great." Dave proceeded, with Paul close behind. "Like sheep to the slaughter" Dave muttered.

"Been nice knowing ya," cackled the duty sergeant.

Dave put his hand on the doorknob, took a deep breath, let it out slowly, and entered the office without knocking. Paul was close on his heels.

Captain Capella didn't look up from his desk and simply said, "Sit." as if ordering a dog to obey. They sat obediently.

"I had a visit today from one of your, ah, associates," Capella began without preamble. He raised his eyebrows at the word 'associates.' "Apparently, the big murder case you two have been working on has been solved, yet I don't have a report on my desk. Why is that I wonder?"

Dave began, "Sir, I can explain."

"No, I don't think you can, actually," replied Capella, his face breaking out in what appeared to be a smile.

Continuing, he asked, "Do you boys know a certain priest named Father D'Angelo."

Stunned, neither detective answered. They just sat there astonished.

"I see that you do," continued the Captain enjoying this immensely.

"How...?" was all Paul could stutter when Capella stopped him.

"Let's just say that you two are not the only folks around here that have friends in high places. Father D'Angelo and I met a long time ago, under, shall we say, special circumstances. When I was a rookie detective, I was working the Mob Desk. I was undercover, when my cover was blown. The mob put a hit out on me. One night I was ambushed, before I knew it, I was shot in the back several times. I knew I was a gonner. I ended up in a private room at Robert Wood Johnson Memorial, surrounded by doctors and a priest. Being a good Catholic, I knew he was there to administer the sacrament of Extreme Unction, or last rites."

Dave and Paul exchanged looks of astonishment. They remained silent as Capella continued.

"Father leaned down and whispered in my ear 'It's not your time, we have need of you,' and so he blessed me and took my hand. The doctors said it was a miracle I survived. I never saw D'Angelo again until this morning, when he came to visit with me and advised me about your case.

Again, they looked at each other yet remained silent.

"Now, I understand that our perp was followed one night by my two best detectives and cornered near the Raritan River Cliffs at the Conservancy. Confronted and trapped, he put up a struggle, resisted arrest, then slipped and fell backwards over the 100-foot cliff, falling to his death on the rocks below. The body must have been washed downstream by the current and into the bay where it was washed out into the expanse of the ocean. I suppose we may never find the body, but the case is closed, and I expect we will hear no more from Shingas."

Once again, silent, the detectives shared a look of astonishment.

"Is that about right, detectives?" asked Capella.

'Yes, Sir. That sums it up precisely," said Dave, careful not to show that his emotions were running wild.

'Good then, now get the hell out of my office and stop wasting my time. I want that report on my desk within the hour." Capella grinned.

"Yes, sir!" came the reply from both detectives as they spun around in their chairs, trying to beat each other out of the room.

When they got back to their desks, they both sat down. Dave shook his head and said to Paul, "What just happened? "

"I would say another miracle."

Before Dave could reply, Dr. Howell entered the precinct, and was directed by the duty sergeant toward the area where Paul and Dave were sitting. She looked beautiful, as always. She had her hair in a braid and wore a slim figure accentuating skirt and loose-fitting blouse, that was obviously designed to give a hint of the curves hidden beneath.

"Hi!" She entered the area where Dave and Paul sat.

"Hi, yourself," Dave replied casually, glad to see her again.

"How have you been?" she asked just as casually, looking directly at Dave trying to draw him out into conversation.

Paul could see that three was one too many, so he politely excused himself. Emily didn't notice Paul's departure, as she was focused on Dave. There was an awkward moment of silence as Dave searched for something to say.

"Actually, we just met with Captain Capella, and ah, well, with a little help from you know who, we closed the big case," replied Dave.

"Great!" she replied with a little more enthusiasm than was required. She was obviously a little nervous. "Perhaps a cause for celebration?" she hinted.

Looking a little scared, Dave swallowed hard, screwed up his courage and asked, "Maybe we could celebrate over dinner?"

"I thought you'd never ask!"

The End Or.....
The
Beginning?